'What now?' she asked.

Her voice was expressionless. But Rico heard the tremor in it. Heard the tightness of her throat. He looked at her. Emotion surged in him again, and he clamped it down yet again.

'We get to a priest,' he said.

She stared at him.

'Why?' The question was a breath, almost inaudible. 'Why do you want to do that?'

'I gave you my word,' he said. 'That's why.' And this was the only way to keep her safe. He met her eyes. They were huge, and strained.

'Thank you,' she said, her voice low, and tight.

Julia James lives in England with her family. Mills & Boon® novels were Julia's first 'grown-up' books as a teenager, alongside Georgette Heyer and Daphne du Maurier, and she's been reading them ever since. Julia adores the English and Celtic countryside, in all its seasons, and is fascinated by all things historical, from castles to cottages. She also has a special love for the Mediterranean—'The most perfect landscape after England!'—and considers both are ideal settings for romance stories. In between writing Julia enjoys walking, gardening, needlework, baking 'extremely gooey chocolate cakes'—and trying to stay fit!

Recent titles by the same author:

PURCHASED FOR REVENGE
FOR PLEASURE...OR MARRIAGE?*
SHACKLED BY DIAMONDS*
BABY OF SHAME

*Models and Millionaires duet

ROYALLY BEDDED, REGALLY WEDDED

BY
JULIA JAMES

First published in Great Britain 2007
Harlequin Mills & Boon Limited,
Eton House, 18-24 Paradise Road, Richmond, Surrey TW9 1SR

© Julia James 2007

ISBN-13: 978 0 263 19556 9
ISBN-10:   0 263 19556 2

Set in Times Roman 10¼ on 11¼ pt
07-0107-54519

Printed and bound in Great Britain
by Antony Rowe Ltd, Chippenham, Wiltshire

ROYALLY BEDDED, REGALLY WEDDED

PROLOGUE

THE dark-haired figure seated at the antique desk and illuminated by an ornate, gold trimmed lamp slapped shut the leather folder, placed it on the growing pile to his right, and reached for yet another folder, opening it with an impatient flick. *Dio*, was there no end to these damned documents? How could so small a place as San Lucenzo generate so many of the things? Everything from officers' commissions to resolutions of the Great Council, all needing to be signed and sealed—by him.

Prince Rico gave a caustic twist of his well-shaped mouth. Perhaps he should be grateful the task seldom came his way. But with his older brother, the Crown Prince, in Scandinavia, representing the House of Ceraldi at a royal wedding, the temporarily indisposed Prince Regnant—their father—had for once been obliged to turn to his younger son to carry out those deputised duties he was generally excluded from.

Rico's eyes darkened for a moment with an old bitterness. Excluded from any involvement in the running of the principality—however tedious or trivial—yet his father still condemned him for the life he perforce led. The twist in his mouth deepened in cynicism. His father might deplore his younger son's well-earned reputation as the Playboy Prince, yet his exploits both in the world of expensive sports like powerboat racing, and on the glittering international social circuit—including the bedrooms of its most beautiful women—generated invaluable publicity for San Lucenzo. And, considering just how much of the principality's revenues derived from it being one of the world's most glamorous locales, his part in contributing to that glamour was not small. Not that either his father or older brother saw it that way. To them, his exploits brought the attention of the paparazzi and the constant risk of scandal— both of which were anathema to the strait-laced Ruling Prince of San Lucenzo and his upright heir.

Not, Rico grudgingly allowed, as he scanned through the document in his hand, that they were not sometimes justified in their concerns. Carina Collingham was an unfortunate instance in that respect—though how he could have been expected to know she was lying when she told him her divorce was through was beyond him.

Despite his instantly having dissociated himself from her the moment he'd discovered the unpalatable truth about the marital status of the film actress, the damage had been done, and now his father had yet another complaint to lay at his younger son's door.

His older brother, Luca, had taken him to task as well, berating him for not having had Carina security-checked adequately before bedding her. Better to exercise some self-restraint when it came to picking women out of the box like so much candy.

'There's safety in numbers,' Rico had replied acerbically. 'While I play the field, no woman thinks she has the ticket on me. Unlike you.' He'd cast a mordant look at his brother, along whose high Ceraldi cheekbones a line had been etched. 'You watch yourself, Luca,' he'd told him. 'Christabel Pasoni has plans for you.'

'Christa's perfectly content with the way things are,' Luca had responded repressively. 'And she does *not* cause a scandal in the press.'

'That's because her fond papa owns so much of it! *Dio*, Luca, can't you damn well ask her to tell *Papa* to instruct his editors to lay off me?'

But Luca had been unsympathetic.

'They wouldn't write about you if they had nothing to write. Don't you think it's time to grow up, Rico, and face your responsibilities?'

Rico's expression had hardened.

'If I had any, I might just do that,' he'd shot back, and walked away.

Well, he'd wanted responsibilities and now he'd got some—signing documents because there was no one else available to do so, and atoning for having had a misplaced affair with a still-technically-married woman.

Maybe if I sign every damn document in my best handwriting before Luca gets back I'll have earned a royal pardon…

But his caustic musing was without humour, and impatiently he scanned the document now in front of him. Something to do with a petition from a convent to be rescinded of the obligation to pay property tax on land on which a hospital had been built in the seventeenth century—a petition which, so the helpful handwritten note appended by his father's equerry reminded him, was nothing more than a *pro forma* request, made annually and granted annually since 1647, requiring nothing more than the customary royal assent. Dutifully, Rico scrawled the royal signature, put down the quill, and reached for the sealing wax, melting the required dark scarlet blob below his name, and then waiting a few moments for it to cool before impressing on it the royal seal. He was just replacing the seal when his phone went.

Not the phone on the desk, but his own mobile—to which very, very few people had the number. Frowning slightly, he slid a long fingered hand inside his jacket pocket and flicked open the handset.

'Rico?'

He recognised the voice at once, and his frown deepened. Whenever Jean-Paul phoned it was seldom good news—certainly not at this late hour of the night. The hour when, Rico knew from experience, the press went to bed. And what a certain section of the press across Europe all too often went to bed with was a story of just who *he* had gone to bed with.

Damn—had the vultures stirred yet more trouble for him over Carina Collingham? Had she been milking the situation for yet more publicity for her career?

'OK, Jean-Paul, tell me the worst,' he said, when foreboding.

The gossip-columnist, who was also the impoverished grandson of a French count, as well as a rare genuine friend in the press, started to speak. But the story that he'd heard was about to break had nothing to do with Carina Collingham. Nothing to do with any of Rico's *affaires*.

'Rico,' said Jean-Paul, and his voice was unusually grave, 'it's about Paolo.'

Rico stilled. Slowly he released his hand from the back of his neck and slipped it down on to the leather surface of the desk. It tensed, unconsciously, into a fist.

'If *anyone*—' his voice was a soft, deadly snarl '—thinks they are going to dig any dirt on him, they are—'

He could hear the wariness in the other man's voice as he interrupted.

'I wouldn't call it dirt, Rico. But I would...' he paused minutely '...call it trouble. Seriously big trouble.'

Emotion splintered through Rico.

'*Dio*, Paolo is *dead*. His broken body got pulled from the wreckage of a car over four years ago.'

Pain stabbed him. Even now he could not bear to think about, to remember, how Paolo—the golden prince, the only one of his father's three sons who had ever won his parents' in-dulgence—had been snuffed out before he was even twenty-two. Like a bright flame extinguished by the dark.

The news had devastated the family. Even Luca had wept openly at the funeral, where the two of them had been the chief pallbearers who had carried their young brother's black-swathed coffin into the cathedral on that unbearable day.

And now, years later, some slimeball hack *dared* to write some kind of sleaze about Paolo.

'What kind of trouble?' he demanded icily. On the desk, his hand fisted more tightly.

There was a distinct pause, as if Jean-Paul were mentally gathering courage. Then he spoke.

'It's about the girl who was in the car crash with him...'

Rico froze.

'What girl?' he asked slowly, as every drop of blood in his veins turned to ice.

Haltingly, Jean-Paul told him.

CHAPTER ONE

*'OH MY darling, oh my darling, oh my darling Benjy-mine—
You are mucky, oh, so mucky, so it's Benjy's bathy-time.'*

Lizzy chirruped away, pushing the laden buggy along the narrow country lane as dusk gathered in the hedgerows. Crows were cawing overhead in the trees near the top of the hill, and the last light of day dwindled in the west, towards the sea, half a mile back down the coombe. It was still only late spring, and primroses gleamed palely in the verges and clustered in the long grass of the lower part of the hedge. The upper part was made of stunted beech, its branches slanted by the prevailing west wind off the Atlantic, which, even now, was combing along the lane and whipping her hair into yet more of a frizz—though she'd fastened it back as tightly as she could. But what did she care about her awful hair, charity shop clothes and total lack of looks? Ben didn't, and he was all she cared about in the world.

'Not *mucky*, Mummy. *Sandy*,' Ben corrected her, craning his head round reprovingly in the buggy.

'Mucky with sand,' compromised Lizzy.

'Keep singing,' instructed Ben.

She obeyed. At least Ben was an uncritical audience. She had no singing voice at all, she knew, but for her four-year-old son that was not a problem. Nor was it a problem that everything he wore, and all his toys—such as they were—came from jumble sales or from charity shops in the local Cornish seaside town.

Nor was it a problem that he had no daddy, like most other children seemed to have.

He's got *me*, and that's all he needs, Lizzy thought fiercely, her hands gripping the buggy handles as she pushed it along up the steepening road, hastening her pace slightly. It was growing late, and therefore dark, but Ben had been enjoying himself so much on the beach, even though it was far too cold yet to swim, that she had stayed later than she had intended.

But its proximity to the beach had been the chief reason that Lizzy had bought the tiny cottage, despite its run-down condition, eleven months ago, after selling her flat in the London suburbs. It was much better to bring a child up in the country.

Her face softened.

Ben. Benedict.

Blessed.

That was what his name meant, and it was true—oh, so true! He had been blessed with life against all the odds, and *she* had been blessed with him. No mother, she knew, could love her child more than she did.

Not even a birth mother.

Grief stabbed at her with a familiar pain. Maria had been so *young*. Far too young to leave home, far too young to be a model, far too young to get pregnant and far too young to die. To be smashed to pieces in a hideous pile-up on a French motorway before she was twenty.

Lizzy's eyes were pierced with sorrow. Maria—so lovely, so pretty. The original golden girl. Her long blonde hair, her wide-set blue eyes and angelic smile. Her slender beauty had been the kind of beauty that turned heads.

And sold clothes.

Their parents had been aghast when Maria had bounded in from school, still in her uniform, and told them that she'd been spotted by a scout for a modelling agency. Lizzy had been despatched to chaperon the eighteen-year-old Maria when she went up to the West End for her try-out shoot. The two girls had reacted very differently to the experience, Lizzy recalled. Maria had been ecstatic, instantly looking completely at home in the fashionable milieu, while Lizzy couldn't have felt more out of place or more awkward—as if she were contaminated by some dreadful disease.

Lizzy knew what that disease was. She'd known it ever since her blue-eyed, golden-haired sister had been born, two years after her, when, overnight, she had become supremely unimportant to her parents. Her sole function had been to look out for Maria. And that was what she'd done. Walked Maria to school, stayed late at clubs Maria had belonged to, helped her with her homework and then, later, with exam revision. Although Maria, being naturally clever, had not, so her parents had often reminded her, needed much help from her—especially as Lizzy's own exam results had hardly been dazzling. But then, who had *expected* them to be dazzling? No one. Just as no one had expected her to make any kind of mark in the world at all. And because of that, and because going to college cost money, Lizzy had not gone to college. The pennies had been put by to see Maria through university.

But all their hopes had been ruined—Maria had been offered a modelling contract. She'd been over the moon, telling her parents that she could always go to university later, and pay for it herself out of her earnings. Her parents had not been pleased, they had looked forward to spending their money on Maria.

'Well, now you can pay for Lizzy to go to college instead,' Maria had said. 'You know she always wanted to go.'

But it had been ridiculous to think of that. At twenty, Lizzy had been too old to be a student, and not nearly bright enough. Besides, they'd needed Lizzy to work in the corner shop that her father owned, in one of London's outer suburbs.

'Lizzy, leave home,' Maria had urged, the first time she'd come back after starting her new career. 'They treat you like a drudge like some kind of lesser mortal. Come up to London and flat with me. It's a hoot, honestly. Loads of fun and parties. I'll get you glammed up, and we can—'

'No.' Lizzy's voice had been sharp.

Maria had meant it kindly. For all her parents' attention to her she had never been spoilt, and her warm, sunny nature had been as genuine as her golden looks. But what she'd suggested would have been unbearable. The thought of being the plain, lumpy older sister dumped in a flat full of teenage models who all looked as beautiful as Maria had been hideous.

But she should have gone, she knew. Had known as soon as that terrible, terrible call had come, summoning her to the hospital in France where Maria had been taken.

If she'd been living with Maria surely she'd have found out about the affair she'd started? Perhaps even been able to stop it? Guilt stabbed her. At least she'd have known who Maria was having an affair *with*.

Which would have meant—she glanced down at Ben's fair head—she would have known who had got her pregnant.

But she did not know and now she would never know.

She paused in her tuneless singing. Further back down the lane she could hear the sound of a car engine. Instinctively she tucked the buggy closer to the verge. There was a passing place further along, but she doubted she could reach it before the approaching vehicle did. Wishing it weren't quite so dusky, she paused, half lifting one set of buggy wheels on to the verge, and warning Ben that a car was coming along.

Headlights cut through the gathering gloom and swept up the lane, followed by a powerful vehicle. It slowed as the lights picked her out, and for a moment Lizzy thought it was going to stop. Then it was past them, and accelerating forward. As it did so, she frowned slightly. The lane she was walking along led inland, whereas the road back to the seaside town ran parallel to the coast. Little traffic came along this lane. Well, maybe the occupants were staying at a farm or a holiday cottage inland. Or maybe they were just lost. She went on pushing the buggy up the final part of the slope, and then around the bend to where her cottage was.

As she finally rounded the curve she saw, to her surprise, that the big four-by-four had parked outside her cottage.

A shiver of apprehension flickered through her. This was a very safe part of the world, compared to the city, but crime wasn't unknown. She slid her hand inside her jacket and flicked her mobile phone on, ready to dial 999 if she had to. As she approached her garden gate she saw two tall figures get out of the car and come towards her. She paused, right by her gate, one hand in her pocket, her finger hovering over the emergency number.

'Are you lost?' she asked politely.

They didn't answer, just closed in on her. Every nerve in her body started to fire. Then, abruptly, one of them spoke.

'Miss Mitchell?'

His voice was deep, and accented. She didn't know what accent. Something foreign, that was all. She looked at him, still with every nerve firing. His face was shadowed in the deepening dusk; she just got an impression of height, of dark eyes— and something else. Something she couldn't put a name to.

Except that it made her say slowly, 'Yes. Why do you want to know?'

Instinctively she moved closer to the buggy, putting herself between it and the strangers.

'Who are those men?' Ben piped up. His little head craned around as he tried to see, because she'd pointed the buggy straight at the gate to the garden.

She heard the man give a rasp in his throat. Then he was speaking again. 'We need to speak to you, Miss Mitchell. About the boy.' There was a frown across his brow, a deep frown, as he looked at her.

'Who are you?' Lizzy's voice was shrill suddenly, infected with fear.

Then the other man, more slightly built, and older, spoke.

'There is no cause for alarm, Miss Mitchell. I am a police officer, and you are perfectly safe. Be assured.'

A police officer? Lizzy stared at him. His voice had the

same accent as the taller, younger man, whose gaze had gone back fixedly to Ben.

'You're not English.'

The first man's eyebrows rose as he turned back to her. 'Of course not,' he said, as if that were a ridiculous observation. Then, with a note of impatience in his voice, he went on, 'Miss Mitchell, we have a great deal to discuss. Please be so good as to go inside. You have my word that you are perfectly safe.'

The other man was reaching forward, pushing open the gate and ushering her along the short path to her front door. Numbly she did as she was bade. Tension and a deep unease were still ripping through her. As she gained the tiny entrance hall of the cottage she paused to unlatch Ben from his safety harness. He struggled out immediately, and turned to survey the two tall men waiting in the doorway to gain entrance.

Lizzy straightened, and flicked on the hall light, surveying the two men herself. As her gaze rested on the younger of the two, she saw he was staring, riveted, at Ben.

There were two other things she registered about him that sent conflicting emotions shooting through her.

The first was, quite simply, that in the stark light of the electric bulb the man staring down at Ben was the most devastatingly good-looking male she'd ever seen.

The second was that he looked terrifyingly like her sister's son.

In shocked slow motion Lizzy helped Ben out of his jacket and boots, then her own, then folded up the buggy and leant it against the wall. Her stomach was tying itself into knots. Oh, God, what was happening? Fear shot through her, and convulsed in her throat.

'This is the way to the kitchen,' announced Ben, and led the way, looking with great interest at these unexpected visitors.

The warmth of the kitchen from the wood-burning range made Lizzy feel breathless, and the room seemed tiny with the two men standing in it. Instinctively she stood behind Ben as he climbed on to a chair to be higher. Both men were still regarding him intently. Fear jerked through her again.

'Look, what *is* this?' she demanded sharply. Her arm came around Ben's shoulder in a protective gesture. The man who looked like Ben turned briefly to the other man, and said something low and rapid in a foreign language.

Italian, she registered. But the recognition did nothing to help her. She didn't understand Italian, and what the man had just said to the other one she'd no idea. But she understood what he said next.

'*Prego,*' he murmured. 'Captain Falieri will look after the boy in another room while we…' he paused heavily '…talk.'

'No.' Her response was automatic. Panicked.

'The boy will be as safe,' said the man heavily, 'as if he had his own personal bodyguard.' He looked down at Ben. 'Have you got any toys? Captain Falieri would like to see them. Will you show them to him? Can you do that?'

'Yes,' said Ben importantly. He scrambled down. Then he glanced at Lizzy. 'May I, please?'

She nodded. Her heart was still pounding as she watched the older man accompany Ben out of the kitchen. Supposing the other man just walked out of the house with Ben. Supposing he drove off with him. Supposing…

'The boy is quite safe. I merely require to talk to you without him hearing at this stage. That much is obvious, I would have thought.'

There was reproof in the voice. As though she were making trouble. Making a nuisance of herself.

She dragged her eyes to him, away from Ben leading the other man into the chilly living room.

He was looking at her from across the table. Again, like a blow to her chest, his resemblance to Ben impacted through her. Ben was fair, and this man was dark, but the features were so similar.

Fear and shock buckled her again.

What if this was Ben's father?

Her stomach churned, his heartbeat racing. Desperately she tried to calm herself.

Even if he's Ben's father he can't take him from me—he can't!

Faintness drummed through her. Her hand clung on to the back of the kitchen chair for strength.

'You are shocked.' The deep, accented voice did not hold reproof any more, but the dark eyes were looking at her assessingly. As if he were deciding whether she really was shocked.

She threw her head back.

'What else did you expect?' she countered.

His eyes pulled away from her and swept the room. Seeing the old-fashioned range, the almost as old-fashioned electric cooker, ancient sink, worn work surfaces and the scrubbed kitchen table standing on old flagstones.

'Not this,' he murmured. Now there was disparagement clear in his voice. His face.

The face that looked so terrifyingly like Ben's.

'Why are you here?' The words burst from her.

The dark eyebrows snapped together. So dark, he was, and yet Ben so fair. And yet despite the difference in colouring, the bones were the same, the features terrifyingly similar.

'Because of the boy, obviously. He cannot remain here.'

She felt the blood drain from her.

'You can't take him. You can't swan in here five years after conceiving him and—'

'What?' The single word was so explosive that it stopped Lizzy dead in her tracks.

For one long, shattering moment he just stared at her with a look of total and utter stupefaction on his face. As if the world completely and absolutely did not make sense. Lizzy stared back. Why was he looking at her like that? As if she were insane. Deranged.

'*I* am not Ben's father.'

The words bit from him. Relief washed through her, knocking the wind out of her. The terror that had been dissolving her stomach—the terror that, for all her defiance, this man invading her home had the power to take Ben from her, or at the very least to demand a presence in her son's life—the fear that had gripped her since she had seen the startling resemblance in their faces, began to subside.

'I am Ben's uncle.' The words were flat. Irrefutable. 'It was my brother, Paolo, who was Ben's father. And, as you must know, Paolo—like your sister Maria, Ben's mother—is dead.' Now his voice was bleak, stark.

Lizzy waited for the flush of relief to go through her again. The man who had got her sister pregnant was dead. He could never threaten her. Could never threaten Ben. She should feel relief at that.

But no such emotion came. Instead, only a terrible empty grief filled her.

Dead. Both dead. Both parents. And suddenly it seemed just so incredibly, blindingly sad. So cruel that Ben had had ripped from him both the people who had created him.

'I'm…I'm sorry,' she heard herself saying, her throat tight suddenly.

For just a moment the expression in his eyes changed, as if just for the briefest second they were both feeling the same emotion, the same grief at such loss. Then, like a door shutting, it was gone.

'I've…I've never known who Ben's father was.' Lizzy's voice was bleak. 'My sister never regained consciousness. She stayed in a coma until Ben was full-term, and then—' She broke off. Something struck her. She looked at the man who looked so much like Ben, who was his uncle. 'Did…did you know about Ben?'

The brows snapped together. 'Of course not. His existence was entirely unknown. That might seem impossible, given the circumstances of his parents' death, which seem to have concealed even from you the identity of his father. However, thanks to the mercenary investigations of a muck-raking journalist, about which thankfully I have been recently informed, his existence is unknown no longer. Which is why—' his voice sharpened, the initial impatience and imperiousness returning '—he must immediately be removed from here.' His mouth pressed tightly a moment. 'We may have located you ahead of the press, but if we can find you, so can they. Which means that both you and the boy must leave with us immediately. A safe house has been organised.'

'What journalist? What do you mean, the press?'

A frown darkened his brow.

'Do not be obtuse. The moment the boy's location is discovered, the press will arrive like a pack of jackals. We must leave immediately.'

Lizzy stared uncomprehendingly. This was insane. What was going on?

'I don't understand. I don't understand any of this. Why would the press come here?'

'To find my nephew. What do you imagine?' Impatience and exasperation were snapping through him.

'But why? What possible interest can the press have in Ben?'

He was staring at her. Staring at her as if she were completely insane.

Across the hall, Ben's piping voice came from the living room, talking about his trainset.

'This is the level crossing, and that's the turntable.'

His voice faded again.

The man who was Ben's uncle was still staring at her. Lizzy started to feel cold seep through her.

'We haven't done anything.' Her voice was thin. 'Why would any journalist be interested in Ben? He's a four-year-old child.'

That look was still in his eye. He stood, quite motionless.

'He was born. That is quite enough. His parentage ensures that.' Exasperated anger suddenly bit through his voice. 'Surely to God you have intelligence enough to understand that?'

Slowly, Lizzy took another careful step backwards. She did

not like being so physically close to this man. It was overpowering, disturbing. Her heart was hammering in her chest.

What did he mean, Ben's parentage? She stared at him. Apart from his being so extraordinarily, devastatingly good-looking, she did not recognise him. He looked like Ben, that was all. A dark version. Very Italian. He must be quite well-off, she registered. The four-by-four was a gleaming brand-new model. And he was wearing expensive clothes; she could see that. He had the sleek, impeccably groomed appearance of someone who wore clothes which, however deceptively casual, had cost a lot of money. And he had that air about him of someone who was used to others jumping to do his bidding. So he could easily be rich.

But why would that bring the press down in droves? Rich Italians were not so unique that the press wrote stories about them.

A frown crossed her face. But what about his brother, Paolo? His dead brother who was Ben's father. Had he been someone the press would be interested in?

He'd said that surely she must know that Paolo was dead. But how should she? She knew nothing about him.

Carefully, very carefully, she spoke.

'My sister was not a supermodel, she was just starting out on her career—just making a name for herself. No journalist would be interested in her. But your brother—the man she…she had a child by. Was he—I don't know—someone well known in Italy? Was he a film star there, or on the television? Or a footballer, a racing driver? Something like that? Some kind of celebrity? Is that what you mean by Ben's parentage?'

She stared at him, a questioning look on her face. Slowly, it changed to one of bewilderment.

He was looking at her as if she were an alien. Fear stabbed her again.

'What—what is it?'

His eyes were boring into her face. As if he were trying to penetrate into her brain.

'This cannot be,' he said flatly. 'It is not possible.'

Lizzy stared. *What* was not possible?

He was holding himself in; she could see it.

'It is not possible that you have just said what you said.' His expression changed, and now he was not talking to her as if she were retarded, but as if she were—unreal. As if this entire exchange were unreal.

'My brother—' he spoke, each word falling as heavy as lead into the space between them '—was Paolo Ceraldi.'

Nothing changed in her expression. She swallowed. 'I'm sorry—the name does not mean anything to me. Perhaps in Italy it might, but—'

A muscle worked in his cheek. His eyes were like black holes.

'Do not, Miss Mitchell, play games with me. That name is *not* unknown to you. It *cannot* be. Nor can the name of San Lucenzo.'

Her face frowned slightly. San Lucenzo? Perhaps that was where Ben's father had come from. But, even if he had, why the big deal?

'That's…that's that place near Italy that's like Monaco. One of those places left over from the Middle Ages.' She spoke cautiously. 'On the Riviera or somewhere. Lots of rich people live there. But…but I'm sorry. The name Paolo Ceraldi still doesn't mean anything to me, so if he was famous there, I'm afraid I just don't—'

The flash in his eyes had come again. With cold, chilling courtesy he spoke, but it was not civil.

'The House of Ceraldi, Miss Mitchell, has ruled San Lucenzo for eight hundred years,' he said sibilantly.

There was silence. Complete silence. Some incredibly complicated arcane equation was trying to work itself out in her brain, but she couldn't do it.

Then the deep, chilling voice came again, icy with a courtesy that was not courteous at all.

'Paolo's father is the Ruling Prince.' He paused, brief and deadly, while his eyes speared hers. 'He is your nephew's grandfather.'

CHAPTER TWO

MIST was rolling in, like thick cotton wool. She felt the room start to swirl around her. Instinctively, she grabbed out with her hand and caught the edge of the kitchen table. She clung on to it.

Not true.

Not true. Not true. Not true.

If she just kept saying it, it would be true. True that it was *not* true. Not true what this man had just said. Because of course it wasn't true. It couldn't be true. It was absurd. Stupid. Impossible. A lie. Some stupid, absurd, impossible lie—or joke. Maybe it was a joke. That must be it. Just a joke. She threw her head back to suck in deep draughts of air. Then she steadied herself, forcibly, and made herself look across at the man who had just said such a stupid, absurd, impossible thing.

'This isn't true.'

Her voice was flat. As flat, she realised, with a hideous, gaping recognition in her guts, as his had been when she'd said she had no idea who...

Ben's father. Ben's father was.

'No.' She'd spoken out loud. Her legs were starting to shake. 'No. This is a joke. It's impossible. It has to be. It's just not possible. I haven't understood it properly.'

'You had better sit down.' The voice was still chill, but less so. Lizzy gazed at him with wide, shock-splintered eyes. Her eyebrows shot together in a frown.

That complicated, arcane equation was still running in her head.

He had just said that Ben's father had been the son of…she forced her mind to say it … the son of the Prince of San Lucenzo. But he had said he was Ben's uncle. His dead father's brother. Which meant that *his* father was also…

She stared. It wasn't possible. It just wasn't possible.

He let her stare. She could see it. Could see he was just standing there while she clung to the edge of the table in the kitchen in her tiny little Cornish cottage where, a few feet away, from her stood.

'I am Enrico Ceraldi,' he enlightened her.

She sat down. Collapsing on the kitchen chair with a heavy thud.

He cast a look at her.

'Did you really not know who I was?' There was almost curiosity in his voice. And something flickered in his eyes.

'Of course I bloody didn't.' The return burst from her lips without her thinking. Then, as if she'd just realised what she'd done, her face stiffened.

'I'm sorry,' she spoke abruptly. 'I didn't mean to be—' She broke off. Something changed in her face again. She lifted her chin, looking directly into his eyes. 'I didn't mean to speak rudely. But, no,' she said heavily, yet still with her chin lifted, 'I did not recognise you. I've heard of you—it would be hard not to have.' Her voice tightened with disapproval. 'But not with the surname, of course. Just your first name and…' she paused, then said it '…your title.'

She got to her feet. The room swayed, but she ignored it. A bomb had exploded in her head, ripping everything to shreds. But she had to cope with it. She straightened her spine.

'I find this very hard to deal with. I'm sure you understand. And I am also sure you understand that I have a great many questions I need to ask. But also—' she held his eyes and spoke resolutely '—I need time to come to terms with this. It is, after all, quite unbelievable.'

She looked at him directly. Refusing to look away.

Long, sooted lashes swept down over his dark eyes. Eyes, she realised, with the now familiar hollowing still going on inside her stomach, that were more used to looking out of photographs in celebrity magazines and the gossip pages of newspapers.

I didn't recognise him. I simply didn't recognise him. He's all over the press and I never recognised him.

But why should I? And why should I think that someone like him could turn up here and tell me that...that Ben is...

Shock kicked through her again.

She bowed her head. It was too much. It was all too much.

'I can't take any more.'

She must have spoken aloud, defeat in her voice.

For one long, hopeless minute she just stared blankly into the eyes of the man standing opposite her. The brother of Ben's father. Who was dead. Who had been the son of the Reigning Prince of San Lucenzo. Who was also the father of the man standing opposite her.

Who was therefore a prince.

Standing in her living room.

'I can't take any more,' she said again.

Rico shifted his head slightly, and glanced behind him as the occasional dazzle of other traffic on the motorway illuminated the interior of the vehicle.

She was asleep. So was the boy. She was holding his hand, reaching out to him in the child seat he was fastened into.

His mouth pressed together and he looked away again, back out over the glowing stream of red tail-lights ahead of him. Beside him, Falieri drove steadily and fast, the big four-by-four eating up the miles.

Rico stared out over the motorway.

Paolo's son. Paolo's son was sitting in the car. A son that none of his family had known about.

How could it have happened?

The question seared through him, as it had done so often since Jean-Paul had told him the story that was set to break in the press. It seemed impossible that Paolo's son should have disappeared, without anyone even knowing of his existence. And yet, in the nightmare of that motorway pile-up in France all those years ago, with smashed cars and smashed bodies, he could see how rescue workers, finding the female occupant of Paolo's car still alive and clearly pregnant, had cut her free first and rushed her to hospital. A different hospital from the one where Paolo's mangled body had been taken hours later, when all those still living had been dealt with.

Cold horror chilled through him. In the carnage no one had made the connection between the two—the dead Prince Paolo Ceraldi and the unknown young woman, comatose and pregnant.

Never to regain consciousness.

Never to tell who had fathered her child.

And so no one had known. No one until some get-lucky hack had decided to see if there was any mileage in a rehash of the tragedy of Paolo's death, and his investigations had turned up, against all the odds, a French fireman who'd mentioned he had freed a woman from the wreckage of the very type of sports car that the journalist knew Paolo Ceraldi had been driving. From that single item the hack had burrowed and burrowed, until he had pieced together the extraordinary, unbelievable story.

How Prince Paolo Ceraldi, dead at twenty-one, had left an orphaned son behind.

The story would blaze across the tabloids.

'Get the boy.'

Luca's urgent command echoed in Rico's head. He'd phoned Luca the moment he'd hung up on Jean-Paul.

'We have to get the boy before the press does,' Luca had said. 'Get Falieri on to it tonight. But, Rico, it's essential we look as if we don't know about the story. If they think we are trying to stop it, they'll run with it immediately. In the meantime—' his voice had hardened '—I will contact Christa. Maybe for once

I will, after all, exact a favour from her father…it won't stifle the story, but it may just delay it. Buy us some time. Enough for Falieri to get the child safely out of their reach.' He'd paused, then gone on, his voice dry. 'It seems, just for once, Rico, that your close proximity to the press has come in handy.'

'Glad to be of use,' Rico had replied, his voice even drier. 'For once.'

'Well, you can really be of use now,' Luca had cut back. 'I can't leave this wedding, if I did it would simply arouse suspicion, so I'm stuck here for the duration. I'm counting on you to hold the fort. But Rico?' His voice had held a warning note in it. 'Leave it to me to tell our father about this debacle, OK? He'll take it a lot better from me.'

Rico hadn't stuck around to find out how his father had taken the news that the Ceraldis were about to face their biggest trial by tabloid yet. He'd had only one imperative. To find Paolo's son.

Emotion buckled him. He'd been holding it back as much as he could, because there had been no time for it. No time to do anything other than get hold of Falieri and track down the child his brother had fathered.

He felt his heart squeeze tightly. It was incredible that here, now, just in the seat behind him, his brother's son was sleeping. It was almost like having Paolo back again.

Debacle, Luca had called it. And Rico knew he was right. He loathed the thought of all the tabloid coverage that was inevitably going to erupt, even with the boy safely with him now, but far more powerful was the sense of wonder and gratitude coursing through him.

He turned in his seat, his eyes resting on the sleeping form of the small boy.

His heart squeezed again. Even in the poor light he could see Paolo's features, see the resemblance. To think that his brother's blood pulsed in those delicate veins, that that small child was his own nephew.

Paolo's son. His brother's child. The brother who had been killed so senselessly, so tragically.

And yet—

He had had a son.

All these years, growing up here, in this foreign country, raised by a woman who was not even his own mother, not knowing who he was.

We didn't know. How could we not have known?

A cold, icy chill went through him.

For a long moment his eyes watched over the sleeping boy, seeing his little chest rise and fall, the long lashes folded down on his fair skin.

Then, slowly, they moved to the figure beside the child seat.

His expression changed, mouth tightening.

This was a complication they could do without.

His gaze rested on her. A frown gathered between his brows. Had she really not realised who he was? It seemed incredible, and yet her shock had been genuine. His frown deepened. He had never before encountered anyone who did not know who he was.

He dragged his mind away. It was irrelevant that his reaction to her evident complete ignorance of his identity had…had what? Irritated him? Piqued him? No, none of those, he asserted to himself. He was merely totally unaccustomed to not being recognised. He had been recognised wherever he went, all his life. Everyone always knew who he was.

So being stared at as if he were the man in the moon had simply been a new experience for him. That was all.

Dio, he dismissed impatiently. What did he care if the girl hadn't realised who he was? It was, as he had said, irrelevant. She knew now. That was all that mattered. And once she'd accepted it—not that the look of glazed shock had left her face until she'd fallen asleep in the vehicle—it had at least had the thankful effect of making her co-operate finally. Silently, numbly, but docilely.

She'd made sandwiches and drinks for herself and Ben,

telling him while he ate that they were going on an adventure, and then heading upstairs to pack. Ben had shown no anxiety, only curiosity and excitement. Rico had done his best to give him an explanation he could understand.

'I...' He had hesitated, then said it, a shaft of emotion going through him as he did so. 'I am your uncle, Ben, and I have only just found out that you live here. So I am taking you on a little holiday. We'll need to leave now, though, and drive in the night.'

It had seemed to suffice.

He had fallen asleep almost instantly, the car having only gone a few miles, and it had not taken a great deal longer for the aunt to fall asleep as well. Rico was glad. A car was not the place for the next conversation they must have.

He glanced at her now, his face tightening in automatic male distaste at the plain-faced female, with her unflattering frizzy hair and even more unflattering nondescript clothes.

She couldn't be more different from Maria Mitchell. She possessed not a scrap of her sister's looks. Maria had been one of those naturally eye-catching blondes, tall and slender, with wide-set blue eyes and a heart-shaped face. No wonder she'd become a model. The photos Falieri had dug up of her had shown exactly how she must have attracted Paolo.

They would have made a golden couple.

Pain bit at him, again. *Dio*, both of them wiped out, their young lives cut short in a crush of metal. But leaving behind a secret legacy.

Rico's eyes went back to his nephew, softening.

We'll take care of you now—don't worry. You're safe with us.

Oblivious, Ben slept on.

Lizzy stirred. Even as the first threads of consciousness returned, she reached automatically across the wide bed.

It was all right. Ben was there. For a moment she let her hand rest on the warm, pyjama-covered back of her son, still fast asleep on the far side of the huge double bed. They were in some kind of private house, at which they'd arrived in the middle of the night—specially rented, and staffed by San Lucenzans flown in from the royal palace, or so she had been told by Captain Falieri. A safe house. Safe from prying journalists.

Disbelief washed through her, as it had done over and over again since that moment when she'd stared at the man who had invaded her cottage and realised who he was.

She was still in shock, she knew. She had to be. Because why else was she so calm? Partly it was for Ben's sake. Above all he must not be upset, or distressed. For his sake she must treat this as normal.

Impossible as that was.

What's going to happen?

The question arrowed through her, bringing a churning anxiety to her stomach.

Was the Prince still here? Or had he left her with Captain Falieri. She hoped he was gone. She was not comfortable with him.

She shifted in her bed. Even had he not been royal, let alone infamous in the press—what did they call him? The Playboy Prince? Was that it?—she could never have been comfortable in his company. No man that good-looking could make her feel anything other than awkward and embarrassed.

Just as, she knew with her usual searing honesty, a man like that could never be comfortable with *her* around. Men like that wanted to be surrounded by beautiful women—women like Maria. Females who were plain and unattractive, as she was, simply didn't exist for them. Hadn't she learnt that lesson early, knowing that for men she was simply invisible? How many times had male eyes slid automatically past her to seek out Maria?

She jerked her mind away from such irrelevancies, back to what she did not want to think about. The paternity of her son.

And his uncle. Prince Enrico Ceraldi.

He won't be here still, she guessed. He'll have left—returned to his palace and his socialite chums. Why would he hang around? He probably only came to the cottage in person because he wanted to check out that Ben really did look like his brother.

She opened her eyes, looking around her. The bedroom was large, and from what she could tell the house was some kind of small, Regency period country house. Presumably sufficiently remote for the press not to find Ben. How long would they need to stay here? she wondered anxiously. The sooner the story broke, the better—because then the fuss would die down and she and Ben could go home.

She frowned. Would Ben be upset that this mysteriously arrived uncle had simply disappeared again? She would far rather he had not known who he was. Her frown etched deeper. Why had he told Ben? It seemed a pointless thing to do. The news story would just be a nine-day wonder, and, although she could understand why the Ceraldi family would want to tuck Ben out of sight while it was going on, there was no need to have told Ben anything.

She'd have to tell Ben that even though Prince Enrico was his uncle, he lived abroad, and that was why he wouldn't see him again.

Even so, it seemed cruel to have told him in the first place. Ben had asked about his father sometimes, and all Lizzy had been able to do was say that it had been someone who had loved the mummy in whose tummy he had grown, but that that mummy had been too ill to say who his daddy was.

For the hundredth time since the bombshell about Maria's lover had fallen, Lizzy felt disbelief wash through her. And a terrible chill. With all the horror of having to rush out to France, to the hospital her mortally injured sister had been taken to, the news that the pile-up had claimed the life of the youngest prince of San Lucenzo had simply passed her by. She had made no connection—how could she have?

And yet he had been Ben's father. Maria had had an affair with Prince Paolo of San Lucenzo. And nobody had known. No one at all.

It was extraordinary, unbelievable. But it was true.

I have to accept it. I have to come to terms with it.

She stared bleakly out over the room. Deliberately, she forced herself to think instead of feel.

It makes no difference. Once all the fuss in the news has died down, we can just go back home. Everything will be the same again. I just have to wait it out, that's all.

Beneath her hand, she could feel Ben start to stir and wake. A rush of emotion went through her.

Nothing would hurt Ben. Nothing. She would keep him safe always. Nothing on this earth would *ever* come between her and the son she adored with all her heart. Ever.

CHAPTER THREE

'GOOD morning.'

Rico walked into the drawing room. Ben was sitting on the floor in the middle of the room, occupied with a pile of brightly coloured building blocks. His aunt was beside him. He nodded brief acknowledgement of her, then turned his attention to Ben.

'What are you making?' he asked his nephew.

'The tallest tower in the world.' Ben announced. 'Come and see.'

Rico did not need an invitation. As his eyes had lit on his nephew, his heart had squeezed. Memories flooded back in. He could remember Paolo being that age.

A shadow fleetingly crossed his eyes. Paolo had been different from Luca and himself. As his adult self, he knew why. Luca had been born the heir. The firstborn Prince, the Crown Prince, the heir apparent, destined to rule San Lucenzo just as their father, Prince Eduardo, had been destined to inherit the throne from his own father a generation earlier. For eight hundred years the Ceraldis had ruled the tiny principality, which had escaped conquest by any of the other Italian states, or even the invading foreign powers that had plagued the Italian peninsula throughout history. Generation after generation of reigning princes had kept San Lucenzo independent—even in this age of European union the principality was still a sovereign state. Some saw it as a time-warped historical anomaly, others merely as a tax haven and a luxury playground for the very rich. But to his father and his older brother it was their inheritance, their destiny.

And it was an inheritance that would always need protection. Not, these days, against foreign powers, or any territorial interests of the Italian state—relations with Italy were excellent. What made San Lucenzo safe was continuity. The continuity of its ruling family. In many ways the principality was the personal fiefdom of the Ceraldis, and yet it was because of that that it retained its independence. Rico accepted that. Without the Ceraldis it would surely have been merged into Italy, just as all the earlier duchies and city states and papal territories had been during the great Risorgimento of the nineteenth century, that had freed Italy from foreign oppression, and united it as a nation.

The Ceraldis were essential to San Lucenzo, and for that reason, it was essential that every reigning prince had an assured heir apparent.

And—Rico's mouth tightened—that the heir apparent had a back up in case of emergency.

The traditional 'heir and a spare'—with himself as the spare.

It was what he had been all his life, growing up knowing that he was simply there in case of disaster. To assure continuity of the Ceraldi line.

But Paolo—ah, Paolo had been different. He had been special to his parents because he'd been an unexpected addition, coming several years after their two older sons. Paolo had had no dynastic function, and so he had been allowed merely to be a boy. A son. A golden boy whose sunny temper had won round even his strait-laced father and his emotionally distant mother.

Which was why his premature death had been all the more tragic, all the more bitter.

Rico hunkered down beside his nephew, taking scant notice of the way his aunt immediately shrank away. Yes, Paolo's son. No doubt about it. No DNA tests would be required; his paternity was undeniable, blazing from every feature. Perhaps there might be a little of his birth mother about him, but one look at him told the world that he was a Ceraldi.

Benedict. That was what he'd been called. And it was a true name for him.

Blessed.

His heart gave that familiar catch again. Yes, he was blessed, all right. He didn't know it yet, but he would. And he was more than blessed—he was a blessing himself.

Because, beyond all the publicity and press coverage and gossip that was going to explode at any moment now, the boy was going to be seen as the blessing he was.

The final consolation to his parents for the son they had lost so tragically.

Lizzy moved backwards across the carpet and lifted herself into a nearby armchair. She had hoped, at the fact that she and Ben had had the breakfast room to themselves, that it meant Prince Enrico had gone.

She wished he had.

She felt excruciatingly awkward with him there. She tried not to look at him, but it was hard not to feel intensely aware of his presence in the room. Even without a drop of royal blood in him he would have been impossible to ignore.

By day he seemed even taller, outlined against the light from the window behind him, and his startling good looks automatically drew her eyes. He was wearing designer jeans, immaculately cut, and an open-necked shirt, clearly handmade. Immediately she felt the full force of just how shabbily she was dressed in comparison. Her cheap chainstore skirt and top had probably cost less than his monogrammed handkerchief.

At least, apart from that brief initial nod in her direction, he wasn't paying any attention to her. It was all on Ben, or helping him build his tower.

Resentment and embarrassment warred within her.

Ben was chattering away confidently, without a trace of

shyness, his smiles sunny. He was like Maria in that, Lizzy knew. Hindsight over the years since her terrible death had made things clearer to her. It had been a miracle that Maria's sunny-tempered nature had not been warped by her upbringing. Despite the way her parents had doted on her, obsessed over her, she really had seemed to escape being spoilt. And yet, for all her sunny nature, she had known what she wanted, and what she'd wanted was to be a model, to live an exciting, glamorous life. And that was what she'd done, smiling happily, ignoring her parents' dismay, and waltzing off to the life she'd wanted.

And the man she'd wanted.

Disbelief was etched through Lizzy for the thousandth time. That Maria had actually had an affair with Prince Paolo of San Lucenzo and none of them had known. Not even his family, let alone hers.

How had they managed it? He must have been very different from his brother. Even though she hadn't recognised Enrico, she'd still heard of him—and of his reputation. The Playboy Prince. Her covert gaze rested on him a second. He certainly had the looks for it, all right. Tall, broad-shouldered, sable-haired, with strong, well-cut, aristocratic features.

And those eyes.

Dark, long-lashed, with flecks of gold in them if you looked deeply. Not that she could—or would.

She looked away. It was completely irrelevant what he looked like. It was nothing to do with her. All she had to be concerned about was how long she and Ben would have to hide here before they could go back home.

Ben had paused in his tower-building. He was looking curiously at his helper.

'Are you really my uncle?'

Immediately Lizzy stiffened.

'Yes,' he answered. He spoke in a very matter of fact way. 'You can call me Tio Rico. That means Uncle Rico. My brother was your father. But he died. It was in the car crash with your mother.'

Ben nodded. 'I was still growing in her tummy. Then I came out, and she died.'

The Prince's eyes were carefully watching his nephew. Lizzy could see as she held her breath.

Please, *please* don't say anything about the royalty stuff. Please.

There was no point Ben knowing. None at all. It wouldn't make sense to him, wouldn't mean anything. One day, when he was much older, she would have to tell him, but till then it was an irrelevance.

Then, to her relief, Ben himself changed the subject.

'We've finished the tower,' he announced. 'What shall we make next?'

He seemed to take it for granted his helper would stick around.

But the Prince got to his feet.

'I'm sorry, Ben. I don't have time. I have to leave very soon, and first I must talk with your aunt.'

He flicked his gaze across to the figure sitting tensely in the armchair. She got to her feet jerkily. Rico found himself regarding her without pleasure.

How could any female look so dire? No figure, no face, and hair like a bush. His eyes flicked away again, and he did not see her face mottle with colour.

'Please come this way,' he said, as he headed towards the door.

He went through into a room that was evidently a library, courteously holding the door open for the aunt, who walked hurriedly past him. He took up a position in front of the fire-place. She stood awkwardly in the middle of the room.

'You had better sit down.'

His voice was cool and remote. Very formal.

Lizzy tensed even more. The ease of manner he'd displayed towards Ben had disappeared completely.

What did he want to talk to her about? Hopefully it would be to tell her how long she and Ben had to stay here. She hoped it would not be long. This was so unsettling for Ben. She wanted to get him home again. Back to normal. Back to the cottage, where she could try to forget all about who Ben's father had been.

She took a seat on the long leather sofa facing the fire about ten feet away. The Prince went on standing. He seemed very tall. Lizzy wished she had remained standing too.

He started to speak.

'I hope you have begun to come to terms with what has transpired. This has been a considerable shock; I acknowledge that.'

'I still can't really believe it,' Lizzy heard herself say, giving voice to her thoughts. 'It just seems so impossible. How on earth did Maria get to meet a prince?'

Prince Enrico arched an eyebrow. 'Not as impossible as you might think. Your sister's career as a model would have taken her into the social circles frequented by my brother.'

She could read his expression quite clearly. Maria's life had been a world away from her own.

'However, now that you are aware of the situation, clearly you will appreciate that the first priority must be Ben's wellbeing.'

Lizzy's expression tightened. Did he think she didn't know that?

'How long are we going to have stay here?'

The question blurted from her.

There was a pause before the Prince answered her. Lizzy didn't care if she'd offended him, or annoyed him by asking a question of him like that. Simply being in the same room with him was just too embarrassing for her to want anything but to minimise the time she had to endure it. Besides, she didn't want to leave Ben on his own any longer than she had to.

'It is expected that the news story will break any day,' Prince Enrico informed her tersely. 'I doubt that it can be put off any longer. As for how long the story will run—' He took a sharp intake of breath. 'That depends on how much the press are fed.'

Lizzy's eyes sparked. Was that some kind of sly remark

about whether *she* would talk to any journalists when she got back home again?

But the Prince was speaking still.

'The press feed off each other, each trying to outdo the other, rehashing each other's stories, then seeking to add their own exclusive "revelation" to milk the story as much as they can, for as long as they can. It's cheap copy.'

There was a bitter note in his voice she would have had to be deaf not to hear. It was obvious he was speaking from experience. For a moment she felt a tinge of sympathy for him, then she pushed it aside. Prince Rico of San Lucenzo had not had his playboy lifestyle forced upon him, and if he didn't like being hounded by the press he shouldn't live the way he did. But Ben was innocent, a small child.

She could feel her fiercely protective maternal instincts take over. Ben was not responsible for his parentage. So Prince Paolo of San Lucenzo had taken a shine to Maria, had an affair with her, and got her pregnant—well, that was not Ben's fault.

'How long will we have to stay here?' she urged again.

'As long as is necessary. I can say no more than that.' His expression changed. 'I am returning to San Lucenzo this morning. I must report on the situation to my father. You and my nephew will stay here. You will be well looked after, naturally, but you will not be allowed to leave the house and gardens.'

Lizzy frowned. 'You don't imagine I *want* to run into any journalists, do you?'

'Nevertheless.' There was a note of implacability in the Prince's voice.

Lizzy looked at him. Did the Ceraldis think that she *wanted* this nightmare to be true? Did they really think she would do anything to make what was already a horrible situation worse by talking to the press?

Well, it didn't matter what Prince Rico or any of the Ceraldi family thought about her intentions. Right now she was in no position to do anything other than accept that she and Ben could not be at home, and she might as well be relieved—if not actually grateful—that the Ceraldis had moved so swiftly to get her and Ben away.

'However—' The Prince had started speaking again, addressing her in that same terse, impersonal tone, but he broke off abruptly. *'Si?'*

His head swivelled to the door, which had opened silently. A man stood there, quite young, but tough and muscular-looking, despite his sober dark suit. He looked like a bodyguard, Lizzy realised. He said something in low, rapid Italian, and the Prince nodded curtly. Then he turned back to Lizzy.

'I am informed my plane is on standby and has air traffic clearance. Excuse me. I must leave.'

Lizzy watched him go. It was frustrating not to know how long she would have to stay here, but presumably not even the San Lucenzan royal family could know exactly what the press would do, or how long it would take for the story to die away.

Her mouth tightened. Had Prince Enrico really implied that she might try and talk to the press herself? It was the very last thing on earth she'd do.

She gave a mental shrug. There was no point her getting angry over it. Royals lived in a goldfish bowl; their wariness was understandable.

She went back to Ben, next door. He seemed to be taking all this in his stride, and she was grateful. Nor did he seem bothered by their enforced incarceration.

He seemed to take the following days in his stride too. They were left very much to themselves. Captain Falieri and the man who was probably Prince Enrico's bodyguard had disappeared as well, and she saw no sign of anyone else in the house except for the efficient Italian-speaking staff.

She was glad of the time to herself. Her mind seemed completely split in two. On the one hand she was as normal as she could be with Ben—playing with him, reading to him, taking him swimming, to his huge excitement, in the covered swimming pool built into a conservatory-style annexe off the main house—but inside her head her thoughts teemed with emotion.

She was still reeling from it all, but she did her best to hide it from Ben. He was, thank heavens, far too young to understand. He took what had happened at face value, absorbing it into his life as naturally as he had anything else, just as when they'd moved to Cornwall. The centre of his life was her, not his surroundings, and providing she was there, everything, for him, was as it should be.

It was inevitable, however, Lizzy acknowledged, that Ben would ask questions about the man who had so unnecessarily told him that he was his uncle.

'Where has he gone?' Ben asked.

'To Italy.' Lizzy told him. 'That's where he lives.'

'Will he come back?'

'I don't think so, Ben.'

Inwardly she cursed the man. Why had he gone and told Ben he was his uncle? Obviously a child would be interested—especially one who had no other relations. But what possible concern was Ben to Prince Enrico, other than being the unfortunate target of a salacious news story which threatened scandal to the San Lucenzan royal family?

Ben frowned. 'Well, what about Captain Fally-eery? Will he come back? He played trains with me.'

Lizzy shook her head. 'I don't think he'll come back either, Ben. He lives in Italy too.' Deliberately, she changed the subject. 'Now, shall we go and have our tea?'

Ben looked at her. 'Is this a hotel, Mummy, where they cook for you?'

She nodded. 'Sort of.' It seemed the easiest explanation to give.

'I like it here,' said Ben decidedly, looking around him approvingly. 'I like the swimming pool. Can we swim again after tea?'

'We'll see,' said Lizzy.

* * *

Rico stood at one of the windows of his apartments in the palace. It gave a dazzling view over the marina, with its brightly lit-up yachts, and the elegant promenade beyond. Paolo's apartments had been nearby, and had enjoyed similar views. His eyes shadowed.

To think that Paolo's young son was alive in England. That he had been there all along, brought up by a woman who did not even know who he was. It seemed incredible.

His thoughts went back to that ramshackle cottage he'd extracted his nephew from. His eyes darkened. It had shocked him to find Paolo's son living in such conditions.

Paolo's son.

He had known it the instant he had set eyes on him. And so he had told Luca.

'There won't be any need for DNA tests,' he'd told him.

'Well, they'll be done anyway. It's necessary.'

Rico had shrugged. He could understand it, but he also knew that when his family saw Ben in the flesh they would know instantly he was Paolo's child.

'And this aunt? What about her?' Luca had gone on.

'Shocked. That's understandable. She really seemed to have no idea at all.' He'd decided not to tell his brother that she'd failed to recognise him. Luca would find that darkly humorous.

'Can't believe her luck, more likely. She's got it made now.' There had been a cynical note in Luca's voice, and Rico frowned in recollection. Ben's aunt had given no indication of any emotion other than disbelief, and dread of the impending news story.

Then Luca had picked up one of the modelling shots of Maria Mitchell that was in the dossier Falieri had compiled, and glanced at it.

'Blonde bimbo like the sister?' he'd asked casually.

Rico had snorted. 'You're joking. Utterly plain.'

His brother had laughed sardonically. 'Well, at least that

should stop the press being interested in her, and that's all to the good. She won't make good copy if she's nothing to look at.'

Rico, his attention half taken by the latest version of a particular super-car that he liked to drive, which was wending its way along the edge of the marina, found himself frowning again at Luca's comment. It was a cruel way to speak about the girl, even if it was true.

He shifted his mind away from her. Ben's aunt was a complication that would be sorted out very soon now.

His father, during a brief interview with him, had made his wishes clear. And his instructions.

'I leave you to handle the matter,' his father had said.

Rico's mouth twisted. He need not take it as a compliment. As Luca had pointed out, 'It has to be you, Rico. You're the only one of us that can come and go freely. And besides—' the sardonic glint had been clear in his brother's eye '—if there's a female in the equation you're the expert—just as well she's plain, mind you. You'll be immune to her.'

He stepped away from the window. The woman who was his nephew's aunt was of no concern to him.

Only his nephew.

The news story on Paolo Ceraldi's unknown son broke the following morning. The lurid exclusive in a French tabloid was instantly picked up, and exactly the kind of media feeding frenzy ensued that his father so deplored. As Rico knew too well from personal experience, when he had been the subject of press attention.

There was nothing to be done about it except ignore it. His father ordered a policy of silence, and to carry on as if nothing had happened. The royal family's public life was not altered in any way. Rico's mother attended her usual opera, ballet and philharmonia performances, his father carried out his customary duties and Luca his. As for himself, he flew down to southern Africa to participate in a gruelling long-distance rally, as he always did at this time of year.

'No comment,' became his only words in half a dozen languages during the checkpoints, and he couldn't wait to get back into the driving seat and head out across the savannah again.

But there was something else he couldn't wait to do either. Get back to his nephew again. He was counting the days.

CHAPTER FOUR

LIZZY walked into the breakfast room and stopped dead. Prince Enrico was sitting at the table.

She'd had absolutely no idea that he was here.

At her side, Ben showed only pleasure.

'Tio Rico! You came back.'

Lizzy watched the Prince lever his long frame upright.

'Of course. Especially to see you.'

Ben's expression perked expectantly.

'Will you play with me?'

'After breakfast. Would you like to go swimming later?'

'Yes, please.'

'Good. Well, let's have breakfast first, shall we?'

He waited pointedly while Lizzy took her place, Ben beside her, before resuming his.

Lizzy watched as Ben chatted to his uncle. Tension laced through her instantly. He must have arrived back late last night. She had heard nothing.

But then she did not stay up late. In the strange, dislocated days she had spent here she had always retired with Ben, after supper, and once he was bathed and asleep she would spend the time in their room reading. The house came with a well-stocked library, and she was grateful for it. She had made a point of not watching television, quite deliberately. She had not wanted to catch anything of whatever the press might be saying by now about her sister and Ben. She didn't want to think about it.

But now, with Prince Enrico sitting at the head of the breakfast table, it all suddenly seemed horribly real again.

Her eyes had gone to him immediately as she'd entered the room—but then it would have been difficult for them to do otherwise, prince or no prince. He was the kind of man that drew all eyes instantly. She felt again that squirming awkwardness go through her, and wished that she and Ben had got up earlier, and so missed this ordeal.

Not that Ben thought it was an ordeal, evidently. He was chatting away with his uncle, and Lizzy felt her mouth tighten with disapproval.

'There is a problem?'

The accented voice was cool. Lizzy realised that Prince Enrico was looking at her.

'Why are you here? Has something happened? Something worse?'

Her voice was staccato, and probably sounded abrupt. She didn't care.

A frowning expression formed on his face.

'Is there more bad news?' Lizzy persisted.

'Other than what was expected? No. Did you not see any of the coverage?'

'No. It was the last thing I wanted to do. But in which case, if nothing worse has happened, why are you here?'

He looked at her. He had that closed expression on his face. Obviously he wasn't used to being spoken to like that, thought Lizzy. But she didn't care. Tension bit in her.

'I am here at the behest of my father. For reasons that must be obvious even to yourself, Miss Mitchell.'

His words were terse.

She looked blank. 'I don't understand.'

His mouth pressed together tightly, and he looked impatiently at her.

'We will discuss this matter later.' He turned his attention back to Ben. Shutting her out.

Dismissing her.

Anxiety and tension warred within her.

How she got through breakfast she did not know. She could not relax, and, although she deplored it, she knew she was grateful that Ben was chattering away to the Prince, making it possible for her to swallow a few morsels of food through a tight throat.

The moment Ben had finished, she got to her feet.

'Come along, Ben,' she said.

'Tio Rico said we'd go swimming,' Ben protested.

'Not straight after eating,' she said quietly. 'You'll get a sore tummy. And anyway, you need to brush your teeth,' she added, steering him out of the room.

As she gained the large hallway, she felt her stomach sink. Oh, God, now what? Why had he come back here? And why should it be *obvious* to her? Nothing was obvious to her. Nothing. Only that she was desperate for all this to be over, and for her to be able to go home with Ben.

But it seemed that she would have to get through another morning here.

After Ben had brushed his teeth they went back down to the drawing room, where Ben's toys were.

Prince Enrico was there before them. Lizzy tensed immediately.

'This is a good train track, Ben,' he said.

Ben trotted forward eagerly. 'My one at home is bigger, because we didn't bring all the pieces. And some of the engines are at home. But I will tell you who these are that I've got here.' He settled himself down by the track and started to regale the Prince, who had hunkered down.

Abruptly, Lizzy snapped her eyes away from the way the material of his immaculately cut trousers strained over powerful thighs.

Oh, God—isn't it bad enough that he's a prince?

She sat herself down on the sofa. Would the man never clear off?

It seemed not. To Lizzy's dismay, he seemed to be settling himself in. She picked up her book. Ben was happily chattering away, talking about his beloved trainset. She tried to concentrate on her book, and failed completely.

After what seemed like for ever, Ben suddenly stood up.

'Is it time to go swimming yet?'

She got to her feet, relieved. 'Good idea. Let's get your things.' She gave an awkward nod to the Prince, who had stood when she did.

She scurried off with Ben. But to her dismay, when they came back downstairs with the swimming kit and went into the pool room, there was already someone in the water.

The Prince's long, lean body cut through the water in a swift crawl, but when he reached the end of the pool he stopped.

'Ah, Ben, there you are,' he said. 'In you come.'

Lizzy stared in horrified fascination. The Prince had half levered himself out of the water, his arms folded down over the edge. She could see the water draining off his torso.

It was smooth, and perfectly muscled, honed like a sportsman.

She tore her eyes away. Ben was scrambling out of his clothes as fast as he could. With gritted teeth she inflated his armbands and slid them over his arms.

'Hurry, hurry,' said Ben, jiggling around. The moment he was fitted, he ran and jumped into the water.

Jerkily, Lizzy picked up his clothes, and went to sit on one of the padded seats that were dotted by the glass wall.

Thank God I wasn't in the water already.

That would have been the ultimate horror. She sat, feeling far too hot in what she was wearing in this sun-heated area, but there was nothing she could do about it. She felt her cheeks grow flushed as she watched Ben playing in the water.

The Prince seemed ludicrously enthusiastic about entertaining a four-year-old child. He ducked and dived and raced, and pounced on Ben like a shark, eliciting squeals of glee.

She felt resentment and anger mounting in her. What was the point? What was the *point* of Prince Enrico doing this? It would just unsettle Ben, that was all. Make him want something that he wasn't going to have.

He hasn't got a father. He hasn't got an uncle. He hasn't got anyone—he's just got me.

And it wasn't fair on him to let him get a taste of what it might be like if he had a father. A father to play with him, to pay attention to him.

Make him laugh the way he was laughing now.

I want to go home. I just want to go home. I want this over. Done with. Forgotten.

Rico helped Ben out of the pool for the last time, and glanced across at where his aunt was sitting. Her face had gone red in the heat, and she looked worse than ever. She also had a face like sour milk.

His brother's words came back to him, half-taunting, half-mocking—which was Luca's usual attitude towards him on this subject.

'*If there's a female in the equation you're the expert—just as well she's plain, mind you. You'll be immune to her.*'

Well, the latter was true. No doubt about that. With a dispassionate mind he could only feel sorry for any female as unattractive as this one. But as someone he actually had to deal with, however briefly, he could do without it. As for the former—well, females of this variety were definitely ones he was not expert in.

He launched himself out of the pool, effortlessly lifting himself on his arms. The boy's aunt had already busied herself wrapping Ben in a towel and getting him dry. He strolled off to get changed himself, in the cabanas provided for the purpose.

His mouth set. The sooner he'd settled the business here and was back in San Lucenzo the better.

But it had been good to start getting to know Ben.
Paolo's son.
His expression softened
I'll make sure he's OK, Paolo—I promise you.

Lunch had been just as much an ordeal as breakfast. Once again, the source of both her concern and her relief had been that Ben had dominated the proceedings, talking nineteen to the dozen to Prince Enrico. All she'd been required to do was sit there and try to eat through a throat that was getting tighter every moment.

What had happened? Why was Prince Enrico back here? He'd said he'd talk to her later—but when was later?

It was after lunch, it transpired. As they left the dining room he turned to her.

'Settle Ben with some toys, if you please. I shall await you in the library.'

'He has a nap after lunch. I'll come down when he's asleep.'

He gave a curt nod, and she took Ben upstairs, nerves jumping.

Typically, Ben took for ever to go to sleep, and her nerves were stretched thin by the time she could finally leave him, curtains closed, door ajar, and head downstairs.

He was, as he had said, in the library. A raft of daily papers, in both English and Italian, were on the low table, and he was sitting in a leather chair perusing *The Times.*

Surely such a respectable newspaper had not carried such a scurrilous story? she wondered.

But the page he was reading seemed to be about international politics. He cast the paper aside and stood up, indicating the chair opposite him, across the hearth of the unlit fire.

'Please sit down.' His voice was cool..

She sat nervously, stomach knoting.

'We must resolve, as a matter of urgency, as I am sure you will appreciate, the matter of my nephew's future.'

Lizzy stared.

'What do you mean?' she said.

A flicker of irritation showed briefly in the dark eyes, then it was suppressed.

'I appreciate,' he said carefully to her—as if, Lizzy thought, she was stupid, 'that the news of Ben's parentage has come as a profound shock to you. Nevertheless, I must ask you to focus on the implications of that discovery. Like yourself, his father's family were, unfortunately, but in the tragic circumstances understandably, equally unaware that Paolo had a son. Now that this is no longer the case, obviously steps will be taken as soon as possible to rectify the situation.'

She was still staring blankly.

'Rectify?' she echoed.

She saw him take a breath. 'Of course. Ben will now make his life in San Lucenzo.'

Cold went down Lizzy's back. She could feel it—as if her spine was turning to ice.

'No.'

The word was instinctive. Automatic.

She saw the Prince's face first tighten, then take on the same expression that it had had when she had failed to recognise him. Disbelieving.

She didn't care. Didn't care about anything. Except to refute, absolutely, what she had just heard him say.

His expression changed, as if he were making a visible effort. Again he addressed her as if she were stupid.

'Miss Mitchell, do you really not understand that your nephew's circumstances have changed now?' His tone, quite blatantly, was patronising, and Lizzy felt her hackles rise through the ice in her spine. 'It is inconceivable that my brother's orphaned son should live anywhere but in his own country.'

She stared at him.

'I can't believe you're saying that,' she cut across him. 'We're going home—back to Cornwall the moment we can. The sooner the better.'

She saw his face tighten.

'That is no longer possible.' His voice was flat. Implacable.

'What do you mean "no longer possible"?' she demanded. Her voice was rising, she could tell, and she could feel the adrenaline churning in her system. 'Ben and I are going home. That's all there is to it.'

'Ben's home will now have to be in San Lucenzo.'

The voice was still flat, still implacable.

'There's no "have to" about it. No *question* of it!'

Dark, long-lashed eyes stared at her.

'Miss Mitchell—are you being deliberately obtuse?' The question was rhetorical, for he plunged straight on. 'There is no going back. Do you not understand that? Your nephew cannot return to the life you gave him. He must come to his own country to live.'

She leant forward, tension in every line of her body.

'This is ridiculous. Absurd,' she responded vehemently. Emotion was surging through her. 'Completely out of the question. I can understand your reaction to the nightmare of this news story, and I have my sympathies for you and your family. If there is one thing I do feel sorry about for royalty, it's that their private lives are raked over by the press—even when they do not conspicuously court such publicity,' she threw in, with a glancing look in her eyes at him that drew an answering flash and a compression of his mouth. But she allowed him no time to interrupt her. 'If anything, Ben's presence in San Lucenzo could only be an further embarrassment to you. Why on earth would your family want to be landed with your late brother's illegitimate child—"love child", as I suppose the tabloids will coyly call him—as an ever-present reminder of his affair with my sister? Look,' she went on, trying to be reasonable, even with the adrenaline running in her like a river in flood, 'if you are worried that I might, God help me, be insane enough to speak to the press at any point in the future, then I'll sign any gagging papers you want. The *only* thing I want for Ben is a happy, unspoilt childhood. He can't help his parentage, and I won't let it affect him adversely.'

He was staring at her again. She wished he wouldn't do that. Not just because his eyes were the most extraordinary she'd ever seen, but because he was looking at her as if she were from another planet.

His mouth tightened. Italian broke from him, angry and incomprehensible.

Then, as if he were making a monumental effort to control his reaction, he spoke again, and she stared wildly at him, stomach churning.

'You do not seem to understand. My brother did *not* have an affair with your sister.'

'But you've just said—' she launched.

His hand shot up, silencing her.

His dark eyes were completely opaque again.

'He married her.'

Lizzy felt her mouth fall open. Her jaw drop like a stone. With numb, unconscious effort she closed it again, then spoke.

'My sister *married* your brother?' Her voice was dazed.

'Yes. The day before their fatal car crash. I have seen the marriage certificate. It is...' he paused '...quite legal. Apparently—' his voice was as dry as sand '—the name Ceraldi was also unknown to the celebrant.'

She got to her feet, staring at him blindly.

'I don't believe it.'

It was denial again. Just the same as when the man standing in front of her had told her he was a royal prince—and so had his brother been.

And if Maria had married him that meant Ben was—

No—no, it could not be. It was impossible. Ben was just... Ben, that was all.

But if her sister had been married to his father, and his father was a prince of San Lucenzo, then Ben...

She sat down. Her legs felt weightless somehow.

'It's not true.' Her voice was faint. Her eyes wide. She stared across at him. 'Please—please say it isn't true. Please.'

Rico looked at her. She could not have meant what she'd just said. No one could. Certainly no woman in her situation could mean it. She had just been told that her nephew was a royal prince. And yet she was begging him to tell her it was not true.

He inhaled sharply.

'It is hardly a subject for jest. And now that you know, you must realise why there is no question but that Ben be brought up in his own country, with his own family.'

Her eyes blazed with sudden fierce light.

'I don't care if you tell me that Ben is the King of Siam. I'm not uprooting him from his own life, from everything he knows. So *what* if he *is* legitimate? Your brother Paolo was the youngest brother, so Ben isn't going to inherit the throne or anything, is he?'

The strident voice grated on Rico's already stretched nerves. The girl's reaction was incomprehensible. Was she particularly un-intelligent? It seemed he would have to spell everything out to her.

'A royal prince of the house of Ceraldi cannot be brought up as a private citizen in a foreign country.' He spoke heavily, hoping to God the damn woman would finally get through her skull what the reality of the situation was. 'He must be raised by his family—'

'*I* am his family.'

Rico's face closed.

'You are his aunt. Nothing more than that. I appreciate that you have worked very hard to raise my brother's son, and—'

Her strident voice interrupted him again. Rico felt his impatience mounting. It was not just her unbelievable pig-head-edness and her exasperating lack of intelligence that got to him, but her appalling habit of cutting across him.

Her eyes were stabbing at him, and she was getting ludi-crously worked up.

'I am Ben's legal guardian. He is solely my responsibility.'

Rico fought for self-control. 'Then, as his legal guardian, you will want the best for him, no? And clearly—' he tried hard to keep the withering sarcasm out of his voice '—Ben's interests will be served by his being raised by his father's family.' And now the sarcasm did creep in. He couldn't stop it, such were the emotions biting through him at the woman's incomprehensible objections. 'Or did you imagine it would be suitable for my brother's son to be raised in a semi-derelict peasant cottage?'

A line of colour leached out across her cheeks, and Rico, despite his mounting temper, felt a stab of regret. She could not help being poor, and she had, after all, done the best she could for Paolo's son, within her means.

But that was irrelevant now. Whether she liked it or not, she had to accept the truth of the matter—the Ceraldis had a new prince, and his place was with them. Swiftly, he moved on. His father had given him full authority to do whatever was necessary to ensure Ben returned to San Lucenzo as soon as possible.

He held up a hand, forestalling any further comeback from her.

'Miss Mitchell—the matter is not open for debate. I make allowances for your sense of shock, but you must face up to the necessity of the situation. My nephew must go to San Lucenzo with the minimum of delay to start his new life. You must see that.'

She shook her head wildly.

'No, I don't. I don't see anything of the sort. You can't possibly think his life should be turned upside down like that.'

Rico pressed his mouth together, willing himself to stay calm.

'And you, Miss Mitchell, cannot possibly think that Ben's life will not be immeasurably better when he is surrounded by his family. What possible justification can you have for your objection? How can you possibly not welcome this? You live in poverty—all that has changed. Changed completely. Have you not realised that?'

His eyes narrowed infinitesimally as he watched for her reaction. But her face just seemed totally blank. Obviously he would need to be blunter, distasteful though it was.

'You will not suffer by the change in Ben's life, Miss Mitchell. You will always be his aunt, and, although Ben's new life will inevitably be vastly different from what he has been used to so far, you will benefit too. It would not be appropriate for my nephew's aunt to live in poverty,' he said carefully, his eyes watching her. 'Therefore generous financial arrangements will be made in your favour, in appreciation for what you have done for my nephew. You have given up four years of your life to look after him—it is only right that your invaluable contribution should be recognised. But now you will be able to resume the life of a young woman, independent of the responsibilities you have had to assume up till now.'

His eyes rested on her as he waited for the penny to drop. But her face was still quite expressionless.

It irritated Rico. Did he have to spell *everything* out in excruciatingly vulgar detail? Evidently so. His mouth tightened. He took a controlled breath, and prepared to speak again.

But before he could say anything she got to her feet.

It was a jerky movement, like an automaton. Her eyes were pinned on his. There was something in them that took him aback. Then she spoke. Her voice was strange.

'You do not seriously think I am going to let you part me from Ben, do you?'

She was trembling like a wire strung out to breaking point. Emotion poured through her, terror and fury storming together. They spilled over into a torrent of words.

'Do you really think I would ever, *ever* allow Ben to be taken from me? Do you? How can you even imagine that for a moment? I'm his *mother*—the only mother he's ever known.'

A burning, punishing breath seared through her lungs. 'Listen to me and listen well. Because I will say this over and over again until I get you to understand it. I am Ben's mother—his guardian. And that means I guard him—I guard him from anything and everything that threatens him, threatens his happiness, his emotional and physical well-being, his long-term stability…*everything*. I love him more than my own life—I could not love him more if he were my birth child. He is all I have left of my sister, and I made a vow to her that I would keep her child safe, that I would be the mother to him that she was not allowed to be. He is my son and I am his mother. It would *devastate* him to be taken from me—how could you even *think* of doing so? Nothing will come between us. I will never let him be taken from me. *Never.'*

Her face was contorted, but she could not stop. She had to make him listen—had to make him hear.

'You must be completely insane to think of taking him from me. How do you even *begin* to think I would consent to it? Consent to Ben losing the only mother he's known. Are you mad, or just evil, even to *think* of separating us? No one takes a child from its mother. *No one.'* She shut her eyes. Her throat was burning, her breath choking. 'Oh, God, how could this nightmare ever have happened. How?'

Her anguished question rang into silence, complete silence. She stood there, shaking like a leaf.

Then, slowly, a voice spoke. Deep and resonant.

'No one will take Ben from you. You have my word.'

Rico was in his bedroom. The phone was against his ear. He stood with one arm extended, resting his hand on the folded wooden shutters that framed the sash windows. From where he stood he could see the gardens. Ben and his aunt were on the lawn, in the last of the early-evening sunshine, playing football. Two goals were roughly marked out with sticks. Ben kicked, and scored, and ran around gleefully in imitation of professional footballers. His aunt threw up her hands in exaggerated defeat, and took a goal kick. It was a very bad one, and Ben returned it instantly, scoring yet another goal. He crowed with triumph.

At the other end of the phone line, Rico's brother was speaking.

'What do you mean, she won't give him up? She's nothing more than his aunt—what claim can she have?'

'A watertight legal one,' replied Rico dryly.

There was a pause. Then Luca spoke.

'She wants more money, I take it?' His voice was sharp.

'She wants her son.' Rico realised his voice was equally sharp.

'The boy is only her *nephew*,' riposted his brother.

'She's raised him as her son, and he regards her as his mother. Which, legally, she is. She adopted him at birth. So, if she does not want to part with him, we have to accept that.'

There was a pause again.

'How much did you offer her?' Luca asked.

'Luca—this is not *about* money. She's not prepared to consider it, OK?' He paused, then spoke again. 'And neither am I any longer. The attachment between them is definitely that of mother and child. I've been with them all day—so far as Paolo's son is concerned, the woman is his mother. There's nothing we can do about that. We may not like it, but that's the way it is. Our only way forward is for her to live in San Lucenzo with the boy. I have to persuade her of that, and I will do my best to do so. But—' he took a sharp breath '—I gave her my word we would not try and take the child from her.'

There was another pause. Outside in the garden Ben was still playing football. Rico felt a sudden urge to go and join in.

Luca was speaking again. 'Rico, do and say nothing for the moment. I'll report this back to our father. He won't like it but...' Rico could almost hear Luca shrug. 'Look, I'll phone you back.'

The line went dead. Rico's gaze dropped again to the figure playing on the lawn below with Ben. She was wearing some kind of grey tracksuit, baggy and shapeless, and her frizzy hair was tied back in an unflattering bunch. She looked overweight and lumpy. She really was extraordinarily unappealing. Yet what did her appearance matter to Ben? Even as he watched, he saw Ben trip as he ran to intercept the ball, and fall sprawlingly on the grass. She was there in an instant, hugging him, inspecting his grass-stained knee, then dropping a kiss on it before resuming play again. An ordinary maternal gesture.

Memory shafted through him. Or rather, lack of it. Who had picked him up when he'd gone sprawling like that? A nanny? Whichever of the nursery floor staff was looking after him at the time? Not his mother. He'd only ever seen his mother at five in the afternoon, when she had taken tea and interviewed both himself and Luca as to their progress in lessons that day.

A frown creased his brow. Paolo had been the only one of them ever to sit beside his mother on the exquisite silk-upholstered sofa in her sitting room. The only one of them he could remember her embracing.

He felt his heart squeeze again. He would bring her Paolo's son.

He glanced at his watch. He doubted Luca would phone back within the hour. Time enough for Rico to teach his nephew some football moves. He headed downstairs.

'It's no good, Ben, it's definitely bedtime.'

'Mummy—one more goal. Just one.'

'Golden goal,' said Rico.

'All right, then,' conceded Lizzy.

She had just passed the strangest half-hour. Out of nowhere, the Prince had emerged on to the lawn and joined in their game of football. Or rather taken it over.

Ben was ecstatic.

'You can ref, Mummy,' he instructed her.

She sat in a heap at the side of the pitch area, and watched. Her emotions were still in turmoil, but at least she was calmer than she had been.

You have my word, he had said.

Did he mean it?

He had seemed different when he'd said that to her. She didn't know why, or how, but he had.

And he'd looked at her. Looked at her into her eyes.

As if she were a real person suddenly.

And something had happened in that look. Something that for the first time had made the hard, fearful knot inside her ease.

Just by a fraction.

Something had changed.

Something had changed as she'd poured out her horror and terror in front of him. Telling him—screaming at him—that she would never let Ben be taken from her, that she was his mother by everything but physical birth. That she would never, ever, let such harm come to him as to be wrested from the only person he knew to be his mother.

Who had been the only person in the world to him.

Until now.

She felt emotion move and shift within her.

A pang went through her. Yes, she was Ben's mother—she would be all her life. Nothing could ever change that.

But now he's got an uncle. Two uncles. And grandparents too.

A family.

A family to whom Ben was not just the embarrassing result of an affair—someone they would wash their hands of, hide away out of sight.

They wanted him. They wanted him because he was the son of their dead son, their dead brother.

Emotion twisted within her.

If they were anything other than what they are, I'd be over-joyed at their discovering Ben's existence.

But that was the trouble. They *were* who they were. It was unbelievable, unreal—and the truth.

Depression rolled over her. Whichever way you looked at it, the whole situation was impossible.

Anguish filled her. There could be no resolution to this. How could there be? Two worlds had collided—the normal world, and the world the Ceraldis lived in. A world that was totally unreal to everyone except themselves.

And Ben was caught in the middle. Crushed between them.

And so was she.

CHAPTER FIVE

Rico stared at his brother. He had been summoned back to San Lucenzo the following morning, and now that he was here Luca had dropped a bombshell on him.

'This is a joke, right? And, as such, it isn't funny.'

The Crown Prince of San Lucenzo looked back at him with dispassionate eyes. He was good at dispassion, thought Rico viciously. Great at dispensing insane ideas as if they were commonplace, obvious no-brainers.

'It would solve the problem we are facing.'

'Are you mad? It's not a question of solving problems—this is about my *life*. And I am *not* about to sacrifice it for the reasons you think I should.'

'It's hardly a permanent sacrifice. Besides, I thought you said you had really taken to the boy.'

Rico's eyes flashed angrily.

'That doesn't mean I have to—'

His brother held up his hand. 'Yes, I understand. But listen, Rico—what other option is there? She's the legal guardian of Paolo's son. She won't relinquish the boy. You're saying that the only way for us to have Paolo's son is to have her as well. But how? We *cannot* have an English unmarried mother, a commoner, whose father kept a shop, living here with legal responsibility for a child who just happens to be our nephew and therefore a royal prince.' His face tightened. 'It will cause serious problems of protocol and security. What I've suggested cuts those problems right out.' Both the tone of his voice and his expression changed. 'I don't have to tell you that your co-operation in this matter would be appreciated by our father.'

He pressed on.

'We're talking a year—eighteen months at the most. That's all, Rico. Enough to serve the proprieties. Make everything watertight.'

His eyes rested on his younger brother.

'You're always talking about having a more active role in affairs. Wanting to take on responsibilities. All your life you've chafed at being the "spare". Well, now you can do something about that. No one else can do this, Rico—only you. You know that. Only you.'

There was an intensity in Luca's gaze that bored into Rico. For a long, endless moment Rico met his brother's eyes. Then, with a curse, he broke away.

'Damn you for this, Luca.'

Luca raised sardonic eyebrows. 'Damn me all you like—but do this for us all,' he retorted coolly.

His brother's voice, when he replied, was even cooler. 'I'll do it for Paolo,' he said.

The sleek, powerful car ate up the miles between the airfield and the rented house. But for Rico it was still too slow. He wanted to drive faster—much faster.

And in the opposite direction.

Instead, he was heading into a cage. He was going to have to put his head into a noose and let it be pulled tight.

His mood was grim. At his side, in the passenger seat, Falieri kept silent. Rico appreciated it. Falieri had been fully briefed, he knew, either by Luca or their father, and he knew exactly what Rico was about to do.

'Tell me I'm insane,' Rico demanded.

'It makes sense, what you are going to do,' Falieri said quietly.

'Does it?' Rico retorted bitterly. 'Keep reminding me of that, will you?'

'You are doing it for the boy,' said Falieri. 'And for your late brother.'

'Keep reminding me of that too—' said Rico.

He slammed on the brakes and changed gear viciously, ready to turn off the road.

Heading into that noose.

Ben greeted him excitedly, rushing to him with a cry of pleasure. Rico scooped him up. The boy's little arms wound around his neck, his sturdy body strong against Rico's chest. The hard, tight band around his lungs seemed to lighten fractionally.

I can do this. I can do it for Paolo. I can do it for Ben.

Gently, he lowered his nephew to the ground again. His eyes slid past him to the figure standing there, looking as out of place as she always did.

Dio, she looked worse than ever. Her skin had gone mottled, and her hair seemed frizzier than ever. She was wearing faded cotton trousers and an ill fitting top.

Revulsion raced through him.

He crushed the instinctive rejection. He'd committed to this course of action and there was no way out now. It might be insane—but he'd said he'd do it.

And there was no point putting it off. He had to do it now, before his feet hardened into ice. So, as he lowered Ben to the floor, he made himself look at her again.

'How have you been?' he asked.

She gave a half-shrug and didn't quite meet his eyes. She never did, he realised. Except that time when she had laid into him about being Ben's legal guardian and never parting from him.

His expression sobered. The intensity of her reaction had shocked him. More than shocked him. It had made him realise, for the first time since discovering about Paolo's son, that it didn't matter that the girl was only Ben's biological aunt—in emotional reality she was much, much more.

And she was right. Completely and indisputably right. To take Ben from her would be an unspeakable cruelty to the child. And to her—and she did not deserve that.

It must have been hard, taking on an orphaned child all on her own, in her circumstances.

'How did your father take it?' She swallowed. 'The fact that I won't let Ben be parted from me?'

He could hear the tension in her voice, like wires around her throat.

He looked at her.

'Another way of resolving the situation has been arrived at.'

Her eyes flashed.

'Anything involving taking Ben from me is—'

He held up a hand, silencing her.

'That will not happen. However,' he spoke heavily, steeling himself to do so, 'this is not the place to discuss this matter.' He cast a speaking look at Ben, who had gone back to his trainset, to rearrange some points. 'Have you dined?'

She pressed her lips together. 'I eat with Ben,' she said. 'It saves the staff doing two meals.'

'Very considerate,' said Rico dryly. 'Well, I have not. So I suggest that I do so while Ben is in his bath and then, when he is asleep, you will appreciate that we cannot postpone any longer a discussion about his future.' He cast a look at her. 'This must be done—none of us has any choice in that.'

Her expression had become strained, and she looked away. Ben piped up, and Rico was grateful.

'I've finished the track now—come and play,' he invited him. 'Let's race engines.'

Rico grinned, his face lightening.

'A race? Then prepare to be beaten, young man.'

For his pains he got a withering look. 'Silly you. I've got the express train,' he told Rico pityingly.

Out of the corner of his eye, Rico saw Ben's aunt slip away. He settled down to play with his nephew. It was a lot easier when she wasn't around.

Then he remembered what he had committed to do, and he felt his heart sink like lead. Even for Paolo's sake, this was going to be excruciating.

Ben was asleep, drifting off even as she finished reading his bedtime story to him. Usually Lizzy just had a bath herself, then read until she fell asleep. Ben woke early, and there was no question of a lie-in. So she never minded early nights.

But tonight she had to go downstairs again.

And face the Prince.

Her stomach knotted itself. She couldn't see what his solution might be—how this nightmare could be resolved.

Round and round her tired head went the drearily familiar litany. Two worlds colliding—no way out. No way out.

She knew only one thing—whatever the Ceraldis wanted, they were not going to part Ben from her. Not while she had breath in her body.

Grimly, she left the door to the bedroom ajar, letting in light from the landing, and then headed downstairs.

She was shown into the drawing room, and the Prince was already there, standing staring out over the near-dark gardens, the curtains undrawn. He had a glass of brandy in his hand, Lizzy registered.

She also registered something else. Something she instantly did her best to suppress. And yet it was impossible.

Impossible for her and every other woman in the world. Impossible to ignore that he was the most drop-dead gorgeous male she'd ever seen.

Embarrassment flushed through her. It seemed wrong to be so aware of his ridiculous good-looks. She had no business being aware of them.

Yet with that brooding expression on his face he just looked even more compelling.

He turned as she advanced into the room, and his eyes rested on her.

Immediately she felt her face mottling, as it always did whenever she came into his eyeline. Making her horribly conscious of her grim appearance.

Yes, I know—I look awful. There's nothing I can do about it. So, please, just don't look at me.

'Won't you sit down?'

Awkwardly, Lizzy lowered herself on to the sofa. She watched the Prince walk across and take a seat opposite her, separated by a large square coffee table. He swirled the brandy slowly in his glass for a moment, staring down into it. Then his head lifted.

He started to speak.

'I know you have found it very hard to accept what has happened,' he began, his voice slow and careful, 'but I hope that the reality of the situation has now finally sunk in. And that you have begun to appreciate that Ben's life cannot continue as it was.'

She opened her mouth to speak, but he hadn't finished.

'Hear me out. Before you say anything, hear me out.' He took a breath. It rasped in his lungs. 'As I said, I understand that it's difficult to accept, but you must—you have no choice. Ben is no longer the boy you thought he was. Whether you like it or not, you cannot deny his heritage. He is my brother's son— the offspring of his marriage to your sister. The circumstances of their deaths are tragic beyond belief, but we must deal with the outcome. And the outcome is Ben—our mutual nephew and your adopted son. This is the reality. And the reality of his paternity is, therefore, that he is a prince. Nothing can change that. Not all the wishing in the world.'

His expression changed. Emotion flared in his eyes suddenly. 'And I do not wish it. I would not wish it for a fraction of a second. Ben is a blessing—a gift from God. My dead brother's son restored to us. No. Do not blanch.' His voice had changed again, become measured and formal. 'Just because he is a gift to us, to my family, it does *not* imply that he is not precious beyond price to you. Or...' He paused, then said deliberately, 'Or you to him. That is not the issue. I gave you my word I would not pursue any avenue of resolution to this situation that was premised upon Ben leaving your care. But...' He paused again, then resumed, with absolute emphasis on each word. 'You *must* accept that his old life has gone. It cannot continue. Ben is a royal prince of the House of Ceraldi. Nothing can change that. His future must be based upon that fact.' He took another sharp intake of breath. 'And that means that he cannot live an ordinary life any more. He must come to San Lucenzo. With you.'

She had gone white, he could see. Her hands were clenched in her lap, and her breathing was uneven. But at least she was not interrupting him. He took another swift mouthful of brandy, feeling the fiery liquid burning in his throat.

He started speaking again.

'There is no easy way out of this situation. But a way does exist. And that is what I am going to propose to you. We have a situation which urgently requires resolution. And there is a way to do so. A drastic way, but nevertheless, in the circumstances, the only way forward.'

He could feel cold pooling in his legs, slowly turning his feet to ice. He had to say this—he had to say this now. Before he cut and ran. Ran as if all the devils in hell were after him.

He stared blankly into the face of the woman sitting opposite him. A woman who was a complete stranger. But to whom he *had* to say the following words.

'We get married,' said Rico.

She didn't move. That was the most unnerving thing of all. She just went on sitting there, hands clenched in her lap, face white. Rico felt his guts tighten. Had he really just said what he had? Had he been *that* insane?

And yet he knew it was not insanity that had made him say the words, but something much worse.

Necessity. Because, loathe Luca as he might for what he had suggested, Rico could see the unavoidable sense of it. The *impasse* they were in was immovable. Ben and his adoptive mother came as a package—that was all there was to it. A package that had to be incorporated somehow—by whatever means, however drastic—into the fabric of the San Lucenzo royal family. Ben alone would have been no problem—but Ben with the woman who had raised him, whom he thought of as his mother and who was in the eyes of the law indeed that person, that was a whole lot more impossible to swallow.

And yet she had to be swallowed. No alternative. No choice.

And he was the one who was going to have to do it. Luca had been right, and Rico hated him for it. But it didn't stop him being right. It would solve everything.

A marriage of convenience—for everyone except himself!

He felt his jaw set even tighter, and unconsciously his hands pressed against the rounded brandy glass. He wanted to take another mouthful, but knew he should not. He'd already drunk wine with dinner, to fortify himself, and although he wanted to drink himself into oblivion he knew it was impossible.

Why wasn't she responding? She hadn't moved—not a muscle. A spurt of anger went through him. Did she imagine this was easy for him? Abruptly he found himself raising the brandy glass anyway, and taking a large mouthful.

Something moved in her eyes minutely.

Then, as if a lever had suddenly been pulled, she jerked to her feet.

'You are,' she said, and there was something wrong with her voice, 'completely mad.'

Rico's eyes darkened. He might have expected this.

'Not mad,' he said repressively, 'just facing facts. Sit down again, if you please.'

She sat. Rico got the feeling it was not to obey him, but

because her legs wouldn't hold her upright. The bones of her face were standing out, and the blood had drained from her skin, which now looked like whey.

'If you marry me,' he began, 'a great many problems simply disappear. We have already established that your old life has gone—there can be no doubt about that. Ben is a royal prince of the House of Ceraldi, and he must be raised as such, in the land of his patrimony. He cannot be raised in this country, and he cannot be raised by you alone. But…' He took an inhalation of breath. 'Were you to marry me, this problem would immediately disappear. You and Ben would be absorbed into the royal family as a unit, and Ben would make the easiest transition possible to his new life. You must see that.'

Her mouth opened, then closed, then opened again.

'No, I don't.'

Rico's mouth pressed tightly.

'I appreciate,' he began, in that same deliberate fashion, 'that you may find this hard to comprehend, let alone accept, but—'

'It's the most insane, tasteless thing I've ever heard.' The words burst from her. 'How can you say it? How can you even *say* it? You can't sit there and say something like that—you *can't*.'

Agitation shook her visibly.

Abruptly he held up a hand.

'It is a matter of expediency, that is all.'

She was staring at him as if he were speaking Chinese. He ploughed on.

'The marriage would take place for no other purpose than to regularise my nephew's existence. As my wife you will become a Ceraldi, with a due place in the royal family, a rank appropriate to the adoptive mother of the Reigning Prince's grandson. You will have a suitable place in all the events of his life. The marriage itself will be a formality, nothing more. Be assured of that.'

There was an edge in his voice, and he continued before she could interrupt him again.

'You may also be assured that the marriage will only be temporary. Once Ben is settled into his new life, and once you are settled into yours, and can move within it in an appropriate manner, then the marriage will be annulled. We will need to observe the proprieties, but my father has agreed that he will sanction a short duration—little more than a year—after which the marriage will have served its purpose and can be dissolved.'

She was still sitting there, looking as if he'd just hit her over the head with a sledgehammer. Well, that was what he *had* done, of course. He, at least, had the last forty-eight hours to accustom himself to what had been proposed as the way through the *impasse*.

'I don't believe that you are saying what I hear you to be saying,' she said very slowly, her voice hollow. 'You cannot be. It's impossible.'

Rico felt anger welling in him, and fought to subdue it.

'I appreciate,' he began again, 'that this is difficult for you to fully take on board, but—'

'Stop saying that. Stop saying I don't understand.' She jerked to her feet again. Her eyes were flaring with emotion. 'What I'm saying is that it's insane. It's *grotesque.*'

Rico's expression froze.

'Grotesque?' The word echoed from him, as though it were in a foreign language. Hauteur filled his face. 'In what way?' he bit out. He got to his feet without realising it, discarding his brandy glass on a side-table as he did so.

She was staring at him wild-eyed, her face working.

'What do you mean, "In what way?"?' she demanded. 'In *every* way. It's grotesque—absolutely grotesque—to think of me marrying you.'

Cold anger filled Rico. To use such a word about such a matter—

He had taken a great deal from this woman, made allowance after allowance for her circumstances, but for her to stand there and tell him that his offer was *grotesque*—

'Would you do me the courtesy of explaining why?' His voice was like ice.

She stared at him. For one long moment she met his gaze, and then, as if in slow motion, he saw her face seem to fracture.

'What else can it be?' she said, in a low, vehement voice.

His voice was stiff with tightly leashed anger. 'I do not see why—'

She cut across him.

'Look at me.'

She stood dead in front of him.

'How can you even think of it? *Look at me.*' Her voice was taut. 'It's *grotesque* to think of me...of me...marrying... marrying...you—'

She broke off. Her head dropped.

Rico stood looking at her. His anger had gone. Vanished. In its place...an emotion he was unused to feeling.

Embarrassment.

And pity.

Then, quietly, he said, 'We'll find another way to sort this out.'

Lizzy lay in bed, but she was not asleep. Beside her, on the far side of the bed, Ben's breathing rose and fell steadily, soundlessly. Lizzy stared into the darkness. Even now, if she did not steel herself, she could feel the hot tide of all-consuming mortification flooding through her. It had been one of those excruciating moments—like a dream in which she found herself walking down the street naked—that she would remember all her life.

How could he have done it? How could he have actually sat there and said that to her face? How could *anyone* in his insane family have thought of it?

She felt a cold sweat break out on her.

Grotesque, she had called it, and that was the only word for it. The very *idea* of someone who looked like her marrying someone who looked like him—for whatever reason.

As if someone were running a sadism course in her mind, she made herself think about it. Made herself see it as if it were real.

Made herself see the headlines. Forced herself to.

The Playboy Prince and the Poison Pill.

Prince Rico and his Bride of Frankenstein.

They'd have a field-day.

She gazed out, wide-eyed and unseeing. Unseeing of anything except the cruel, unforgiving reflection that greeted her every day of her life.

Then, juxtaposed beside it, the image of Prince Rico Ceraldi.

The contrast was…grotesque.

She shut her eyes, as if to banish the image in her head.

All her life she'd known that she was not just unattractive, but actively repellent. It was a harsh word, but it was true. She had proof of it, day after day. She'd learnt to see it in men's eyes—that instant dismissal and rejection.

It was the exact opposite of the reaction Maria had got. Maria, with her tall, slim figure and her lovely face, her long golden hair.

Lizzy hadn't been jealous. What would have been the point? Maria had been the beautiful sister, she the plain one. It was the way it had always been.

Maria, in her kindness, had offered to try and do something to improve her appearance, but Lizzy had never let her. It would have been too embarrassing. Even worse than looking so repellent naturally would have been trying not to, trying to do something about it—and failing.

Because of course she would have failed.

'You can't make a silk purse out of a sow's ear,' her mother would say to her, her mouth pressing tightly in displeasure as she looked over her older daughter.

So she had never tried. She had accepted herself for what she was.

Totally without the slightest attraction to the male sex.

And with Ben it just didn't matter. What did a child care if its mother was ugly? For Ben, it was her love for him that counted, her devotion to him. All he needed from her was her care and her hugs. That was all.

Ben.

Instinctively she reached out her hand and touched his folded little body, lightly brushing his hair before taking her hand away again.

Anguish filled her.

I want to go home. I want to go back home, to Cornwall—I want this nightmare never to have happened. Please, please let it not have happened. Please.

But her prayers were hopeless. The nightmare *had* happened, and she was caught in it. She would never be free of it.

Heaviness crushed her.

'We'll find another way to sort this out,' the Prince had said.

But what other way? The Ceraldis must have been desperate to even entertain what he had come up with—a temporary marriage of convenience to turn her into a princess and therefore a suitable mother for Prince Eduardo's grandson.

The weight on her chest intensified.

I'm nothing but a nuisance to them...

Then she rallied. Tough. Tough that she was nothing but a nuisance to the San Lucenzan royal family. Tough that she was a problem that had to be solved. Tough that their precious grandson just happened to come encumbered by a stand-in mother.

I don't care—I don't care about them, or what an inconvenience I am! I don't care about anything except Ben and his happiness. Ben needs me...and that's all that matters. And for him I'll do anything—anything at all.

Except marry his uncle.

Rico stood under the shower and let the stinging needles of water pound down over his head.

He should be feeling relieved. He should be feeling like a

condemned man reprieved. But he wasn't. An uncomfortable, writhing emotion twisted within him.

He kept hearing that word in his mind.

Grotesque.

How could any woman say that about herself? Feel that about herself?

OK, she was plain. But that was not her fault. So why did she seem to flay herself so for it?

A cynical voice spoke in his head.

She's just facing up to the truth, that's all. No man will ever want her, and she knows that. She knows just what an unlikely couple the two of you would make—the talking behind her back, the whispering, the scornful looks, the offers to comfort you for your affliction in having had to marry such a female.

He silenced the voice. Ruthlessly.

Instead, deliberately, he called another image to mind. The way she was with Ben. Endlessly patient, always loving and affectionate, supportive and encouraging.

She'd brought him up well.

More than well.

He frowned. It must have been hard for her.

She could have so much easier a life now. If he could just get her to see that.

He cut the water off and stepped out of the shower.

OK, so maybe it wasn't ideal having Ben's mother floating around San Lucenzo like a loose cannon. But even if she was a commoner, and an Englishwoman, so what? Something could be sorted, surely? Yes, it would make life awkward—but too bad. Wasn't Paolo's son worth some degree of inconvenience, some rearrangement of protocol and expectation?

He whipped a towel around his lean, honed body, then grabbed a hand towel to roughly pat his hair dry.

Once she and Ben were in San Lucenzo she would start to see for herself how a new life there would be possible. And he would have to make Luca and his father realise that somehow they had to set up a situation where Ben and his mother could live there.

His mind raced on. They didn't have to live in the palace, or the capital itself. The Ceraldis owned enough property in the principality—one of their numerous residences would prove suitable.

A villa by the sea—they'd like that.

He could see Ben in his mind's eye, playing on the beach— a warmer, less windy beach than the one in Cornwall.

I could visit him a lot then. Get to know him. Spend time with him.

Another thought came to him as he shrugged on a bathrobe and discarded the towels.

I'll get something done about her—for her. With good clothes, a decent haircut, make-up—surely she'd look better?

It would be a kindness to her.

He headed for bed, feeling virtuous.

And finally relieved.

CHAPTER SIX

THE jet was starting its descent. Rico could feel the alteration in pitch.

'We're starting to go down, Ben,' he announced.

Ben, captivated, stared out of the porthole, at the tiny patch-work of fields and valleys and rivers spread below. He had taken the journey in his stride so far—and so, to Rico's relief, had his mother.

'Will you at least agree to a visit?' he had asked her the next day. 'Nothing more than that. To allow my parents and brother to meet Ben.' His voice had changed. 'I do not have to tell you how much they long to meet him at last. Please do not deny them that,' he'd finished quietly. 'It will be a very emotional moment for them.'

She had nodded. Something seemed to have changed between them. He didn't know what, but somehow it was easier to talk to her. She, too, and he was sure it was not just his imag-ination, seemed less tense, less awkward in his presence.

Maybe, he thought sombrely, the scene that night had brought everything to a head.

Whatever it was, he was grateful. Grateful that she had agreed to move forward, even in this circumspect way, that she finally seemed to have moved beyond the stonewalling denial that had made her so difficult to deal with.

He had spoken to Luca that morning, telling him they were

going to fly out the following day. What he hadn't told him was that it was only for a visit, not permanently. He would tell Luca privately that there could be no question of a marriage of convenience. That the situation would have to be resolved differently, in a way that Ben's adopted mother was comfortable with.

Luca had not been communicative, had merely wanted to know that Ben was finally on his way and when they would be landing. He'd seemed tense, preoccupied.

Well, it had been a stressful time, Rico acknowledged. Their father was not an easy man, and Rico had sympathy for Luca being the one to bear the brunt of it. However much of a miracle Ben's existence was, it had come with a price tag—one that his father hated to pay. The focus of the world's tabloid press on his family's private affairs.

The stewardess came forward into the cabin to request they put their seat belts on. Rico smiled reassuringly across at Ben's mother. She seemed outwardly calm, but he wondered how real it was.

Ben simply seemed excited.

Ironically, thought Rico, Ben seemed a lot more excited about flying in a plane than he did about the news, broken to him tactfully and carefully the previous afternoon by his uncle and his aunt, that he was, in fact, a royal prince.

'Will I have a crown?' had been his only question, and, when a negative answer had been returned to him, had lost interest in the matter.

His interest in royalty was revived momentarily when they transferred to the car waiting for them at the airfield. The car was flying a colourful standard from its bonnet, and Ben wanted to know why.

'It's your grandfather's flag,' Rico answered. 'Because he's the Ruler of San Lucenzo. We are going to meet him. And your grandmother and your other uncle. The one I told you about yesterday.'

The car glided off. Ben chattered away to Rico, asking him

question after question. Beside him, Lizzy sat, willing herself to stay calm.

But it was hard.

In England, cocooned in the safe house, it had been hard to appreciate the reality of Ben's patrimony. Now that they were here, in San Lucenzo itself, it was suddenly all too real. Fear and apprehension gouged at her, and she could feel her muscles tensing.

She was so completely out of place here. It had been bad enough in England, in that country house, but boarding a private San Lucenzan-registered jet, flying in luxury, with the stewardess saying 'Highness' to Ben's uncle every time she opened her mouth, and a uniformed airfield commander greeting them as they deplaned, and now a bodyguard, Gianni, sitting next to a peak-capped chauffeur driving them in the sleek, official-looking limo with the royal standard on it… It was all telling her that this was a world to which she did not belong.

A world as alien to her as if she'd landed on another planet.

Anxiety and nerves bit through her with merciless pincers.

'It will be all right. Trust me.'

Prince Rico had spoken in a low voice, but there was a note of consideration…kindness, even…that she was not used to. Perhaps it was simply because she was finally doing what the Ceraldis wanted her to do—bringing Ben out to San Lucenzo to meet his royal relatives.

But it seemed more than that.

And Lizzy knew why.

He's sorry for me. He's sorry for me because he knows that I know that the insane idea of a marriage of convenience was just grotesque.

His kindness should have made her feel more embarrassed than ever. And yet, strangely, it seemed to achieve the opposite.

She looked across at him, to where he was patiently answering Ben's questions. Ben was completely at ease with him now—and Rico with Ben, Lizzy could see. He was warm and affectionate, open and demonstrative with his nephew.

It brought a reassurance to her that she badly needed.

If he's like that with Ben, it means his parents and his brother will be too. OK, so they happen to be royalty—but what does that matter in the end? They want Ben to love, because they loved his father, and that's all that matters.

It would be all right—she had to believe that. It would be all right.

And if it wasn't—well. She took a heavy inhalation of breath as she reminded herself she had committed to nothing in coming out here. Ben, like her, was a British citizen, and she was his legal guardian. Nothing happened to him without her consent.

Her eyes went to Ben's uncle again.

Besides, he had given her his word.

He, a royal prince, wouldn't give that lightly or trivially. When he gave it, he would mean it.

Her reassurance deepened.

The windows of the car were tinted, so that although the occupants could see out, no one could see in.

'They are used to the cars of the royal family on the roads,' Rico remarked, as the car wound its slow way through the narrow streets of the city towards the royal palace.

'Does anyone else know we are coming here?' asked Lizzy.

Rico shook his head.

'The pavements would be mobbed with paparazzi if they knew,' he said. 'So far as the press is concerned, you and Ben are still in England. Eventually there will be an official statement from the palace, confirming both Ben's existence and yours, and also officially recognising him as Prince Paolo's son and a member of the royal family. But my father will not be hustled into making any announcements in reaction to the recent stories.'

'So no one knows we're here?' said Lizzy.

'No, you are quite safe. It will be a completely private visit.'

Her tension eased a fraction.

But not by much. The car was already approaching the wide gates of a palace, driving across its wide-paved concourse. The sugar-white, *faux*-castellated royal palace looked as if it was made out of children's candy, Lizzy thought. And the flanking guards were in picturesque antique costume and helmets as they swept past them and into the inner courtyard.

The car drew to a halt in front of a huge double door at the rear of the cobbled courtyard. As it stopped the doors were thrown open and two footmen emerged. One came to open the car door.

Prince Rico got out first, then turned to help lift Ben out and offer his hand to Lizzy. She managed to get out of the car without taking it.

As she straightened, she felt the warmth of the Mediterranean air in her lungs after the air-conditioned car.

Then they were heading indoors, and the cool of marble floors enveloped her as she walked beside Ben, his uncle on his other side, across the wide expanse of an entrance hall.

I'm in a palace, thought Lizzy, and the thought seemed bizarre and unreal.

One of the footmen was processing in front of them, the other bringing up the rear. Ben was still asking Rico questions. Lizzy glanced covertly either side of her, at the ornate walls, with alcoves inset with statuary.

Ahead was a huge flight of stairs, carpeted in royal blue. Prince Rico ascended lithely.

This is his home—he must do this every day of his life.

Her sense of unreality deepened.

So did the sense of oppression that had started to weigh her down.

How could she ever move in this world, even if only on the edges, as the legal mother of the Ruling Prince's grandson? It was impossible.

Grotesque...

The cruel word pincered at her.

They gained the top of the stairs, and a wide landing that

seemed to stretch endlessly in either direction. Off its length sets of double doors marched away.

Everywhere was marble and gilt, and there was the kind of hush that went with a deserted museum.

A man stepped forward, out of a doorway she hadn't even noticed.

The procession halted, and the man bowed briefly to Prince Rico, dismissing the footmen. The man was wearing a suit, and was clearly not a servant but one of the royal staff.

What were they called? Lizzy found herself wondering. Equerries? Was that it?

The man, who was quite young, and wearing pale spectacles which obscured his eyes, was addressing Prince Rico. His glance had gone briefly to Ben, but not to herself.

What am I? Invisible?

The caustic thought merely made her unease deepen.

Prince Rico was frowning, saying something in a sharp voice in Italian to the man. The man's expression did not change, remaining impassive. Unreadable.

Prince Rico turned towards Lizzy, shutting out the other man.

'My father and mother would like to meet Ben on his own for the first time,' he said to her. 'Please do not take offence at this. Were you to be there, they would be constrained to be formal, to behave as the protocols dictate. I hope you will understand?'

Fear flared in her eyes. Then, to her astonishment, her hand was taken.

'It will be all right. You have my word.'

His hands were warm across hers. His eyes, as he looked into hers, were rich with sympathy.

'Trust me,' he said in a low voice. 'Do not be afraid.'

Slowly, very slowly, she nodded. There seemed to be a lump in her throat.

He let go of her hand.

'You will be shown to your apartments, where you can

refresh yourself. I will bring Ben to you. In the meantime, rest and relax. Then, when I've brought Ben back, I will show you around.'

He glanced down at Ben.

'We're going to meet your grandparents now, Ben, and your other uncle. Your mother is going to have a little rest, and then we'll go exploring. There's a lot to see in this palace.' He bent forward conspiratorially. 'Even a secret passage.'

Ben's eyes widened. He slipped his hand into his uncle's, and Prince Rico started to walk off with him, still talking to him.

Lizzy watched them go.

'*Signorina?*'

It was the equerry, or whoever he was.

'I will show you to your new quarters,' said the man.

Numbly, Lizzy followed after him.

Tension netted her like a web.

Rico looked about him and frowned. His parents' private sitting room, which he'd just been ushered into with Ben, was deserted. Yet he'd been told to present Ben immediately. So where was everyone?

'Rico—finally.'

He turned abruptly. Luca had walked in from one of the antechambers. His brother's eyes went swiftly from himself to the small figure holding Rico's hand. For a moment he said nothing, just looked. Then he spoke.

'Yes—difficult to deny his paternity. Far too much Paolo in him.' His eyes flicked back to Rico. 'We were beginning to think you'd never get him here,' he said. 'You must be slipping.' A jibing note entered his voice. 'For a man who can charm any woman he wants into bed in the blink of an eye, it should have been a piece of cake for you to get the boy's aunt eating out of your hand.'

'Cut the sniping, Luca,' said Rico. His voice was sharper than usual. 'Where are the parents?'

His brother's eyebrows rose with a sardonic curve.

'It's Grand Council today—you know our father's never late for those sessions. And as for our fond mama, she always goes back to Andovaria for her fortnight's spa this time of year—had you forgotten?'

Rico stared. '*What?* Di Finori told me Ben had been summoned immediately.'

'Well, of course,' Luca responded impatiently. 'We've had to wait long enough to get him. But—' his mouth pressed '—at least we've got him now.' His voice changed again. 'So we can all relax finally. Especially you.' The jibing note was back in his voice. 'Poor Rico—actually reduced to offering to make the ultimate sacrifice—marriage. And to *such* a bride. I've just checked her out on the security cameras. *Dio*, if I'd known she was that bad even *I* might have thought twice before I did that number on you. Still, it did the business—as I knew it would. She must have snapped your hand off the minute you trotted out the marriage-of-convenience fairytale.'

'You never intended me to go through with it?' Rico's voice was edged like a knife.

Luca gave a laugh, abruptly cut off. 'Thump me one if you want, Rico, but you gave us no choice. I had to be convincing. I had to make sure you believed you were going to have to go through with it.' His mouth thinned. 'Why the hell you gave this Lizzy Mitchell your word that you wouldn't try and take the boy from her is beyond me. That's not something to lie about. That's why I didn't want to put you in a position where you knew you were lying about a marriage of convenience.'

The expression in Rico's eyes flickered minutely. 'I gave her my word to get her to trust me,' he said.

'Bad move.' Luca shook his head. 'You'll be glad to know I didn't mention it to our father—it wouldn't have gone down well. Still, like I said, everything's worked out finally. And now we can finally get this damn mess sorted.'

His eyes went to Ben, who had a blank, confused look on his face at all the incomprehensible Italian being spoken over his head, then to his brother again. For a moment Rico thought he saw something in Luca's eyes. Then it was gone. His voice, when he spoke next, was brisk and businesslike.

'The boy's personal household has been selected, and they're waiting to take him now. He'll have apartments here in the palace to begin with, where security is tighter. Later he'll be moved out to somewhere more remote—up in the hills, probably, to keep him out of circulation. Boarding school's a possibility when he's older, but that's a few years ahead yet. For the moment it's just a question of nannies and tutors. And keeping his profile as low as possible, of course. Everything necessary will be done to mitigate the situation and minimise his presence.' His expression changed again, and he gave a short, angry rasp. '*Dio*, what an ungodly mess! It's been hell dealing with it here, I can tell you!'

'I had the feeling,' Rico said, his eyes narrowing, 'that the idea of a grandson was welcome.'

Luca laughed shortly without humour.

'You've been reading too much of that trash in the press. Yes, of course that's the line the hacks took—they would, wouldn't they? All cloying sentimentality. You don't seriously imagine that our parents would *ever* welcome the news that Paolo had disgraced himself—and us all—by going and impregnating some two-cent bimbo and then *marrying* her?'

Rico gave a shrug. 'Could be worse—the bimbo could still be alive. As it is, it's just the frump of an aunt. What happens to *her* now, by the way?' His voice was offhand.

'Secure apartment here, in the south tower—she's being taken there now—then she'll be deported as *persona non grata* to the principality. Once outside the borders she can do what she wants. She won't get the boy back. Even if the press bankroll any counter-custody claim by her for the publicity, it will take years. While she had the boy and they were still in the

UK we were hamstrung—the law was weighted in her favour. But now it's a different story. We have possession, and that's what counts. She's finished. And you, my dear brother—' Luca clapped him on the back, his slate eyes sparking with his familiar sardonic expression '—are finally off-duty. You're free to celebrate a job well done. Mission accomplished.'

'Not quite,' said Rico.

His right hand slipped from Ben's, fisted, and landed on his brother's left temple with the full weight of his body behind the blow. Luca crumpled, unconscious, to the floor.

Ben had given a gasp, but Rico just took his hand again and started to hurry towards the door.

'Change of plan, Ben,' said Rico.

His voice was tight with fury.

The corridors seemed endless. Like a twisting maze. Numbly, Lizzy followed behind the bespectacled equerry. He said nothing to her, and walked at a pace that was slightly too fast for her. They went up stairs, and along more corridors, and then more stairs, leading upwards.

The décor was getting less palatial with every corridor. Finally he took her through a set of doors and into one more corridor. Lizzy looked about her. This wasn't just less palatial— this was…unused. It was the only word for it. A faint sheen of dust was on the floor, the skirting boards, and the air had a musty smell to it.

'Signorina?'

The equerry, or whoever he was, had opened a door and was waiting for her to go in. She hesitated a moment, then, not knowing what else to do, went in. It was more like a room in a budget hotel than a palace, with a plain bed and furniture, and a small and not very clean window that, Lizzy could see, over-looked some kind of delivery area.

Her suitcase was standing on a slightly frayed rug beside the bed.

It was a single bed, she noticed, frowning slightly, and she glanced around towards the door into what she presumed must be Ben's bedroom. But when she opened it it was only a small, windowless shower room, with no further door leading out of it. She turned.

'Where is my son's bedroom?' she asked. There was sharpness in her voice.

But it was wasted.

The door to the corridor was closing, and as it did she heard a distinct click.

A spurt of alarm went through her, and she hurried to the door, twisting the handle urgently.

It was locked.

The corridor was dingy, clearly disused. Emotion stabbed at Rico, and he suppressed it. There was no time for emotion now. None at all. Methodically he walked along the length of the corridor, testing each handle. Each one yielded to an empty room. They must have been servants' quarters at some point.

The fifth door refused to yield. He paused a moment, listening. There was no sound. Had she tried to scream? Or would she have realised it was bound to be pointless? No one would hear her here.

Emotion stabbed again, like a hornet stinging him. He suppressed it once more. He felt the strength of the lock with his hand, twisting the handle, then stepped back.

It hurt. In films it never looked as if it did. But the jarring pain in his shoulder as the door cracked was irrelevant.

What was not was the huddled figure on the bed. She had just launched up into a sitting position, he could tell.

Even from the shattered doorway he could see the look of terror on her face.

And the streaks of tears.

Her face contorted. Contorted into rage. Fury. Incandescent despair.

'I've got Ben—let's go.' He spoke urgently. 'We have no time—come now. *Now.*' His eyes bored at her. *'Trust me.'*

He could see the emotion in her face. An emotion that he never, ever wanted to see again on a woman's face. Then, abruptly, she hurled herself forward.

'Where is he?'

'At the end of the corridor, keeping watch. He thinks it's a game. He's not upset—he didn't realise what was happening. Don't ask questions—we've got *one* chance to get out of here, and that's all.'

How long would Luca stay out cold? He had no idea. He only knew that precious minutes were ticking by. He seemed to be divided into two people. One of them was raging with fury—the other was deadly calm. It was the latter he kept uppermost.

'Ben—' Her cry was almost a scream, but stifled in her throat.

Rico saw the child turn from his position at the end of the corridor.

'Mummy—come on.' He beckoned her furiously, his little face alight with excitement.

The palace was labyrinthine, but Rico knew it like the back of his hand. Knew exactly which levels were most likely to be deserted. He walked rapidly, blood pounding, her suitcase in one hand and Ben's hand in the other. Ben trotted beside him, his mother behind him, both instructed not to talk, not to ask questions. He mustn't think, mustn't feel. Just keep moving. Fast, urgent. Undetected. Every corner was a risk—someone, anyone, could be there.

But there was no one. No one right up to the service door to his own apartments. Ungently, he shoved Ben and his mother inside even as he yanked out his mobile phone and punched a number.

Thank God Gianni was there, in position. He'd phoned him the moment he'd left his brother out cold on the floor, to give him instructions. He snapped the phone shut and turned to Ben.

'Time for the secret passage,' he said.

Ben's mouth opened wide in wonder.

'Here it is,' said Rico. He'd crossed to the wall into which a fireplace had been set, and felt for the concealed button that operated the door mechanism. He hadn't used it in a while, but it still worked, if creakingly, revealing a narrow entrance to an even narrower staircase.

He gave a sudden grin, his mood lightening for a nanosecond.

'It's the reason I chose these apartments as a teenager. It was a great way to evade curfew. Come on.'

Ben needed no second invitation. He surged forward, his expression blissful, and Rico had to hold him while he flicked on the interior light, got them all inside, and then shut the door.

The concealed staircase opened into a side street in the palace precincts. The car was waiting, its tinted windows closed. Even so, he made his nephew and his mother lie on the floor of the back seat.

'Drive,' he instructed Gianni.

Only as he sat back in his seat, Ben excitedly clutching at his leg and asking him if it were another adventure, did the emotions start to come through.

The violence of them shook him to the core.

They made it to the border in under twenty minutes. He'd debated between speed via the coastal *autostrada* versus heading for the hills, and had gone for the former. He had to take a gamble, and it was absolutely vital they get on to Italian soil.

As they passed through the unmanned border he spoke.

'We're out,' he said. He leant down to haul up Ben, followed by his mother. She busied herself with seat-belts.

'What now?' she asked. Her voice was expressionless, but Rico heard the tremor in it. Heard the tightness of her throat. Heard the fear. The terror.

He looked at her. The chalky complexion, the bones stark

in her face. Emotion surged in him, and he clamped it down yet again.

'We get to a priest,' he said.

CHAPTER SEVEN

THE savage irony of it was that she still balked at marrying him. In the end he had to be brutal.

'It is the only way I can protect you. Protect Ben.'

She stared at him, her face a web of fear.

'It's another trick. A trap.' Her voice was hollow.

'*No*, I swear it. I swear I did not know what they were planning—I swear. If I could, I would get you back to England—but I can't. I've got you into Italy, and now you are safer, because my father will have to work through the Italian authorities and that will slow him down. But if you try and return to England you'll be taken into custody. I can't even get you into Switzerland. All the Italian borders will be watched. And don't think my father won't be able to do it—he'll have some charge against you trumped up. It doesn't matter what—it matters only to prevent you taking Ben back to the UK. You'll be separated, and there'll be some kind of court order taking him into care—something. Anything. Whatever it takes to separate you. And he'll find a way to keep you separated.'

He took a searing breath. 'The only way I can keep you safe is by doing what I've just said. Once we're married they can't touch you, and they can't touch Ben. Neither legally nor because of the publicity. They will have to accept a *fait accompli*. I know my father—he won't risk an open break with me. He won't cause that kind of scandal.'

He looked at her as she sat, her arm tight around Ben, who had lolled off to sleep with the motion of the car, steadily being driven further north towards the alpine foothills. 'I'm the only person who can protect you—keep you and Ben together.'

She stared at him.

'Why?' The question was a breath, almost inaudible. 'Why do you want to do that?'

It echoed through him, reverberating through his being.

Why? She had asked why.

'I gave you my word,' he said. 'Not to let Ben be parted from you. That's why.'

In his head he heard again Luca's voice, describing the nightmare childhood that had been planned for Ben.

Anger blinded him.

Anger at his father, his mother, his brother…the whole damn, twisted, duplicitous, hard-hearted, *callous* lot of them.

How could they do it? How could they even think it?

But he knew how. To them, the only important thing was duty and reputation, avoiding scandal, awkwardness, embarrassment.

And to achieve that they were prepared to take a four-year-old child and wrench it from its mother—trick the mother into coming here in good faith and then throw her out like a piece of rubbish.

His eyes went to her, went to her arm so tight around Ben, and to Ben, his head resting on her side, his hand lying in her lap. Mother and child.

Genetically she might only be his aunt, but to Ben she was everything—the whole world. So what if she were some ordinary member of the masses, utterly unfit to be a royal princess, the mother of a royal prince?

His lips pressed together. And so what that she was utterly unlike any woman he would have chosen for his wife? A woman who knew that brutal, cruel truth…

Grotesque.

That was what she thought a marriage between them would be.

Grotesque. The word tolled through him again.

Shaming him.

Shaming him with its pitiless honesty.

Well, now it didn't matter. Didn't matter what either of them thought about such a marriage. Because neither of them was important now—only Ben.

And this was the only way to keep him safe.

Savage humour filled him. So Luca had set him up like a patsy, had he? Despatching him to mount a charm offensive on Ben's aunt that would steal her child from her, duping him into offering to marry her simply to lull her into a false sense of security. His mouth tightened.

Thanks for the idea, Luca—it's a really good one.

And it would beat his family on all points.

And keep Ben safe with his mother.

His eyes went to the boy. He was still asleep, lolling against his mother.

He met her eyes. They were huge, strained.

'Thank you,' she said, her voice low and tight.

She felt as if she was falling. Falling very far, into a deep, bottomless pit. All she had to cling to was Ben. And it was imperative she did. Imperative she keep hold of him, never, ever to loosen her hold on him—because otherwise he would fall away from her and be lost for ever.

Fear shot through her like a grid of hot wires in her veins. Over and over again the horror of what had happened in the palace, when she had realised she had been locked in that room, when she had realised that it could mean only one thing, still drenched through her.

Her eyes went to the man standing beside her in the chill, stone-built church, his expression drawn and shuttered.

Trust me, he had said.

I give you my word, he had said.

Could she trust him? Was he really rescuing her? Or simply tricking her again?

But how could he be tricking her? He was prepared to do something that would change his life for ever. Something so drastic that it made her feel faint with the enormity of it. He had disobeyed his father, knocked his own brother out cold so he could rescue her, so he could get Ben and her away to freedom...safety.

Safety with him.

He's doing it for Ben. Because he knows it would be unspeakably cruel for him to lose me. And that was why she'd do it too. For Ben.

Nothing else mattered.

The priest was starting to speak. The dimly lit, tiny white-washed church, scarcely more than a chapel, was in a small village somewhere in the hills. She had no idea where. There had been a low-voiced, urgent conversation in the car between the Prince and his bodyguard, who was, so it seemed, not merely loyal enough to his employer to have stood by him, but also possessed of a great-uncle who was a priest.

A frail, elderly man, he stood before them now, clasping their hands together with his and intoning words she did not understand, but which, she knew, were binding her in holy matrimony to the man at her side.

She went on falling.

It was done. Ben and his mother were safe. Relief sluiced through Rico. As he thanked the priest, mentally vowing that he would take every measure to avoid the man getting into the slightest trouble over what he had done, and thanked the housekeeper who had been the witness to the ceremony along with Gianni, Rico knew that there was one more thing to be done.

He ushered Ben and his mother back into the car. Gianni slid into the driver's seat. He knew where to go, what to do.

'I'm hungry,' announced Ben. He had woken up, stood beside Gianni during the brief, hurried ceremony, passively accepting, as children did, without comprehension, what was happening to the grown-ups around him.

'We'll have some food soon—very soon, I promise,' Rico said, ruffling his hair. It was still not quite dark, but they had a way to drive. He would have preferred to fly, but that was out. There was no way he could take a helicopter up without air traffic control knowing about it. But they would head cross country, by obscure routes if they could.

This car was different anyway—a lot less conspicuous. Gianni had fixed the swap—the guy was heading for an all-time bonus. Now he came up trumps yet again.

'You like pizza?' he asked, and passed back a large, double wrapped plastic bag. 'Cold, but good. From my great-uncle's housekeeper, for the *bambino*.'

Ben's face lit.

'Yes, please,' he said.

Rico watched as his mother unwrapped the food and handed it with some paper towels to his nephew, who tucked in hungrily. As they ate, he slid his hand into his pocket and took out his phone. It took a while to be answered, but when it was, he wasted no time.

'Jean-Paul, I've got a story for you…'

The conversation was lengthy, in rapid French, and when he disconnected Rico felt another wave of relief go through him. He also felt anxious eyes on him. He turned his head.

'That was a friend of mine. The one who alerted me that there was a story building about Paolo's long-lost son. He's a good friend, and I trust him absolutely. I've told him we've just got married. That we're making a family for Ben. He'll sit on the story until I give him the word to run with it. That's the weapon I can hold over my father. I'll give him some time to come round, to accept what's happened, but if he stonewalls then Jean-Paul can run the story the way I've given it to him— without any co-operation from the palace. That's the only choice my father gets.'

His voice was grim as he finished.

He slid the phone into his jacket pocket again.

'I still cannot believe that my father did what he did. I knew he was not sentimental about Luca and myself, but Paolo—Paolo was different.' His eyes slid away into the past as he spoke, his voice low. 'Paolo was the one son my parents could treat not as a prince, but as...as a child. As someone in his own right. Someone without a royal function. Who could just be himself. That's why—' His voice halted a moment, then he went on. 'That's why I thought they really wanted Ben. Because he's Paolo's son. I thought they would...' He swallowed. 'I thought they would love him. Love him enough to know that what was important for Ben was what should be done. Love him enough to know that *you* were important to him.'

His eyes looked troubled. 'I am ashamed of them. Ashamed of what they did to you.'

Suddenly, out of nowhere, he touched her arm. Lightly. Just for a moment.

'And I am ashamed of myself as well.'

Lizzy's expression was troubled.

'You're taking the fall for this,' she said, and her voice was low and strained. 'I'm sorry—I'm really, really sorry that you had to...had to do what you've just done. I'll try...I'll try not to be—' She swallowed, then fell silent.

What could she say? *I'll try not to be too grotesque a wife to you?* She felt her throat tightening.

He was silent a moment. Then he spoke.

'It will work out. For all the reasons I told you in England, when I believed that this marriage was what my father wanted. All those reasons are still true.'

She could not reply. What could she say?

That the reason for her refusing him in England was still the same as well?

Well, it was too late for that.

The car drove on into the night. At her side, Ben finished

his pizza. She cleared away the remains, then let him cuddle against her and fall asleep. His little body was warm and sturdy, and her love for him flooded through her.

I've done the right thing. I've done the only thing. The only thing possible to keep him safe.

Her eyes met his uncle's, on the other side of Ben.

A strange emotion pricked through him.

He had done what he had had to do. No other course of action had been possible—anything else had been unthinkable.

I did what I had to do. That is all.

It was my duty.

Duty. But of a different type.

Carrying, strangely, no burden of resentment. Only relief.

Relief that he had done, if nothing else, the right thing. By Paolo, by his son, and by the girl whom he now protected. Who had no one but him to do so. The strange emotion quickened. Quite different from all the emotions that had stormed through him since Jean-Paul's first phone call to him, which seemed now to have been a long, long time ago. He tried to think what the emotion was, to identify it. Then it came to him.

It was a sense of purpose. Doing something that mattered.

A new emotion for him.

'Where are we?' Lizzy's voice sounded bleary, even to her own ears. She had been roused from heavy, uneasy sleep as the car had come to a stop. She straightened up, feeling stiff. Ben was still slouched heavily against her, fast asleep.

'Capo d'Angeli. Jean-Paul has hired a villa here for us. We can stay here as long as we want. No one will disturb us.'

She let him undo the safety catch and she scooped the sleeping Ben into her arms, while Gianni helped her out of the car. A cool breeze came in the night, and all she could make out was a house with a gravelled drive immediately beneath her feet, and a front door opening. She heard Italian spoken, and then she and Ben were being ushered inside. There were people, more Italian, but she was too tired to do anything other than carry Ben upstairs, following the tall, besuited figure ascending in front of her, blocking out of her head everything except the overriding need to get to bed. Get back to sleep.

Like a zombie, she followed him into a room—a large bedroom with a larger bed. A maid was turning it down on either side. She hurried forward to help Lizzy, and within a few minutes—blessedly so—Lizzy was laying her head down on the pillow beside her sleeping son, her eyelids closing.

She wanted to sleep for ever and never wake up. Never face up to what she had just done.

Married Prince Enrico of San Lucenzo.

Downstairs, Rico took out his mobile once more, and pressed the number he knew he had to call.

Luca answered immediately. His voice was taut with fury. Incomprehension. Rico cut him off in mid-denunciation. He called his brother a word he had never used to him before. It silenced Luca long enough for Rico to tell him the new situation. Then, slowly, in a different voice, his older brother spoke again.

'Rico—it's not too late. We'll send a helicopter, and you and the boy can be back here by morning. We'll fix an instant annulment. The girl can be taken care of—we can get her deported from Italy. We can—'

'Wrong again.' Rico's voice was a tight, vicious drawl. 'All you and our father can do is—' He gave instructions that were crude—and anatomically impossible. 'And now, if you please, you can inform my revered father that I am going to start my honeymoon, with my bride and my new son. And there is *nothing* you can do about it. Do you understand me? Nothing. They are in my care now. Mine. And if you had a shred of honour in you, you would never speak to our father again.'

He hung up.

* * *

Lizzy was dreaming. She was back in that hospital, with her sister. But her sister was not in a coma. Instead she was sitting up, cradling a baby, her golden hair like a veil. There was someone else sitting on the bed—a young man with blond hair. They were both fixated on the baby in Maria's arms. They didn't see Lizzy. Didn't even look up.

Then her parents were coming into the ward. They walked past Lizzy, their arms full of presents wrapped up in baby blue. She tried to walk forward, but she couldn't. She had a present for the baby, but there was only room to put the present on the end of the bed. It slid onto the floor. Her mother looked round sharply.

'What are you doing here?' she demanded. 'Maria doesn't need you. No one needs you. And no one wants you either.'

She reached for the curtain and drew it around Maria's bed. Shutting Lizzy out.

Lizzy woke up.

Guilt drenched through her.

She had taken something that was not hers to take. Something she'd had no right to. She turned her head. Ben was asleep on the far side of the huge double bed, his little figure swathed in the light coverlet. Ben—her sister's son. Not hers. Not hers at all.

Anguish filled her. Her hand reached to him, touching his hair. Soft and golden. Like his mother's. His father's.

Not like hers at all.

Not mine. Not mine. Not mine.

The litany rang through her head.

And now she had taken something else she'd had no right to take. Something else she didn't deserve.

And yet she knew bitterly that the theft had come with its own punishment. Heat flushed through her—the heat of mortification. *Grotesque*, she had called the very idea of a marriage between them, the two most opposite people in the world. And yet she had gone ahead with it. She had inflicted herself on him because there was no other way to keep safe the child she had taken from her sister. The child she had no right to. No right to love the way she did.

She felt Ben stir and wake. His eyes opened. Trusting. Instantly content to see her. Knowing that if she was there, then all was well.

Cold iced along her veins. It had so very nearly been different.

I could have been on my way back to England—deported. Ben imprisoned in that palace, never to see me again.

The horror of what had so nearly been consumed her.

Prince Rico had saved them.

Guilt stabbed at her again. He had saved them—and she had repaid him by chaining him to her.

'Mummy?'

Ben was sitting up.

'Is it getting-up time?' he asked brightly. 'Is Tio Rico here?' He looked around expectantly, then, in a puzzled voice, 'Where are we, Mummy? Have we gone back to the palace again?'

She shook her head. A steely hardness filled her.

'No, darling. We're not going back there.' She threw back the bedclothes. 'Come on, let's find out where breakfast is. I'm starving.'

She looked around her. The room was large and airy, and filled with sunlight diffused through bleached wood Venetian blinds. The furniture was simple, but elegant, the walls white, the floor tiled. She found her spirits lifting.

Capo d'Angeli. She had heard of it vaguely, but nothing more. A place where rich people went, but not flash or sophisticated. Discreet and classy. An exclusive, luxury resort on the Italian coast where there were no hotels, only villas, with large private grounds, each nestled into its own place on the rocky promontory overlooking the sea.

Someone had brought up her suitcase. There was not a great deal in it—even less than she'd taken from Cornwall—but there was enough to serve. Ben fell with a cry of pleasure upon his teddy bear, as well as a clutch of his favourite engines.

It did not take long to dress, and when they were both ready

Lizzy drew up the Venetian blinds. French windows were behind them, and a wide terrace, and beyond the terrace—

'Mummy—the sea! It's bluer than my paintbox. Much bluer than home.'

Lizzy opened the French windows and warm air flooded in like an embrace. Ben rushed out, clutching the stone balustrade and staring eagerly out over the tops of the pine trees set below, out to the cerulean sea beyond, sparkling in the morning light.

'Do you think there's a beach?' he asked, his voice pitched with excitement.

'Definitely a beach, Ben.'

The voice that answered him was not hers. It came from further down the terrace, where an ironwork table was set out under a large blue-striped parasol. The table was set with breakfast things, but Lizzy had no eyes for them. All she had eyes for was the man sitting in the pool of shade.

She felt her stomach clench. Oh, God, he just looked so fantastic. He was wearing a bathrobe, and its whiteness contrasted dramatically with the warm tan of his skin tones, the deep vee of the crossover revealing a smooth, hard surface that she flicked her eyes away from jerkily. Not that it did any good to look at any other part of him. His forearms were bare, too, the sleeves of the robe rolled up, and his damp hair was feathering in the warmth. As for his face—

She felt her stomach clench again. He was a ludicrously attractive male, and up to now she'd only seen him in formal attire. Seeing him like this, fresh from his shower, was…

Different.

Completely, utterly different.

And he seemed different too. The tension that had been in him throughout their time together at the safe house, culminating in the extreme emotion of their flight from the palace had gone. Disappeared.

Now he seemed…relaxed.

Carefree.

Ben was running forward. 'Tio Rico, can we go down to the beach?' he asked eagerly.

His uncle laughed. Lizzy's stomach churned yet again. The laughter lit his face, indenting lines around his mouth, lifting his eyes, showing the white of his teeth. Making him look a hundred times more gorgeous. A hundred times sexier—

Oh, God, how am I going to cope with this?

Misery filled her, and with horrible self-conscious awkwardness she walked forward. As she approached, he got to his feet.

'Buon giorno,' he said. There was still a smile in his eyes. Left over from Ben, obviously.

Lizzy swallowed, and gave a sort of half nod. She couldn't look at him—not look him in the eye and know that last night, in some unreal, disorientating, panicked ceremony, she had become this man's wife.

She pulled out a chair and sat down.

'Did you sleep well?' There seemed to be genuine enquiry in his voice.

She swallowed, and nodded again. Jerkily she reached for a jug of orange juice and began to pour herself a glass. Ben was chattering away to his uncle.

His stepfather? A stepfather who could take him away from her—

The breath tightened in Lizzy's throat as the realisation hit her. It was followed by panic. Blind, gut-wrenching panic. Was this another trick? A trap like the one that had brought her to San Lucenzo, with one object only, to take Ben from her?

'Don't look like that.' His voice was low, but it penetrated her panic. Her eyes snapped up. Locked with his. 'It will be all right. *It will be all right.* There is no need for you to fear anything now.'

She felt her throat tighten unbearably.

'Trust me,' he said.

His dark eyes were looking into hers. 'I promised you,' he said slowly, clearly, as if to a frightened child, 'that I will keep you and Ben safe, together, for as long as is necessary. I will *never* allow you to be separated from him. You have my word.'

And slowly, very slowly, Lizzy felt the panic still, the fear drain from her. He held her eyes for one moment longer, and then, with a slight, humorously resigned twist to his lips, he turned to Ben, who was tugging at his sleeve to get his attention back and find out whether he could get down to the beach right away.

'Breakfast first, young man,' he said. 'Then we'll go exploring. When I've got some clothes.' He looked across at Lizzy, who was sipping her orange juice. 'I am having some new clothes sent up to the villa. They should be here soon. The palace may send my own on; they may not. In the meantime, the on-site boutiques by the marina here can supply whatever we want.' His eyes flicked to her and Ben. 'They'll get you two sorted out as well.'

'Oh, no—please. I'm sure I can cope with what I've brought,' Lizzy said hurriedly.

'That will not be necessary.' His expression stilled a moment. 'I know this is hard for you, but everything is different. However…' his voice changed again '…today we shall spend very quietly, giving us time to get used to what has happened. I think we deserve some calm after the storm, no? So, tell me, what do you think of the villa?'

'It's unbelievably beautiful,' Lizzy said.

Rico nodded. 'I agree. Jean-Paul chose well. It's also one of the most remote villas on the Capo D'Angeli estate. Not that we need to worry. Security on the whole estate is draconian. Everyone who stays here wants privacy above all—even from each other. And by the same token,' he said reassuringly, 'you do not need to worry about the staff. They are used to all guests wanting absolute discretion. We can relax completely here—I have even sent Gianni off to take a well-deserved holiday.'

He smiled encouragingly.

On cue a manservant appeared, bearing a tray of fresh coffee and breakfast rolls. Ben needed no encouragement, and was swiftly tucking in.

'He seems to have taken it all in his stride,' said Rico contemplatively. 'I think he will like it here.' He glanced across at Lizzy. 'I think we will like it here.'

She met his eyes. It was getting easier. Not easy, but easier.

'Thank you,' she said, in a low, intense voice. 'Thank you for what you have done.'

'We did what we had to do. There was no other way. No other choice. And now—' his expression changed '—I want to hear no more on it. We have been through a great deal—we deserve a holiday. And this is a good place for one.'

He grinned suddenly, and yet again Lizzy felt that hopelessly inappropriate reaction. She crushed it as much as she could, but dread went through her. How was she going to cope? It was impossible—just impossible.

She steeled herself. Prince Rico was going to have to cope, and so was she. If he could use his upbringing to handle any situation, then she would too. She would force herself.

'What…what will happen today?' she ventured.

'Today? Today we take things easy. Ben must go down to the beach—we'll have a revolution on our hands if we don't take him. The cove at the base of the villa gardens is private to us, so we will not be disturbed. There is a swimming pool here too, of course, on the level below this one. As for toys—well, the villa comes with a fully stocked children's playroom, and for anything else the internet is a great provider. So, you see, we shall have everything we need for the perfect holiday.'

He smiled at her again, then turned his attention to Ben.

'How are you at building sandcastles?' he asked him.

'Really good,' said Ben enthusiastically. 'At home we build them when the tide comes in, and then we make big walls to stop the waves. But the waves always win in the end.'

Rico made a face. 'Alas, there is no tide here—the Mediterranean sea is too small for tides. And the waves are very small too. But the water is lovely and warm. You won't get cold. We can go on a boat, too.'

'Today?' demanded Ben.

'Not today. Perhaps tomorrow. We'll see.'

Ben's expression darkened. '"We'll see" means no,' he said gloomily.

'It means I don't know yet. This is a holiday, Ben. We're going to take it one day at a time. Isn't that right?'

Rico's eyes suddenly flicked to hers.

'One day at a time,' he repeated. 'For us too.'

For a long moment he held her eyes, then Ben reclaimed his attention with yet another question.

She needed time, Rico knew. So much had happened to her since he'd showed up at her ramshackle cottage in Cornwall. And for her, he had to appreciate, it had all been bad. The life she'd known had been ripped away from her. For her, there was no going back.

A surge of determination went through him.

I'll make that life better now. All the fear and trauma is over now.

His eyes flickered over her fleetingly, without her knowledge, as she poured herself more coffee.

I don't believe she has to look this bad. I just don't.

Covertly he studied her. It was hard to see much of her figure, as even in this warmth she was wearing a long-sleeved baggy top that seemed to flow shapelessly into long baggy cotton trousers. Both garments were cheap and worn. She dressed for comfort, not style, that much had always been apparent, but the perpetual bagginess of her clothing made it hard to judge just what her figure really was. She was no stick-thin model, that was for sure, but how overweight was she *really*? And even so, well-cut clothes could conceal a multitude of evils, surely…?

He moved on to try and evaluate her features. That was hard to do too. The unsightly frizz of her hair which, even when tied back as it was now, still seemed to straggle round her face, drew all the attention. He tried to imagine her face without it. It was difficult, he realised, to judge it accurately. The heavy eyebrows didn't help, of course, and nor did the pallid skin. But there wasn't anything actively disastrous—her nose was straight, her jaw defined, her eyes grey, her teeth not protruding or uneven. It was just that her features seemed so completely—nondescript.

Would she look better with make-up? Surely she must? Women always did, didn't they? Not that he was used to seeing women without make-up—make-up and hundreds of euros' worth of grooming, and thousands of euros' worth of clothes and accessories.

Well, now she could have that kind of money spent on *her*. Money was not going to be a problem for her from now on. He would lavish it on her.

His mouth tightened abruptly. In his head he heard Luca's sneering at the sight of her. Anger bit him. Who the hell was Luca to sneer at a woman who had taken her dead sister's child and dedicated her life to raising him? Being a single mother on little money was no ride in the park—certainly not a limo-ride. And so what if she weren't beautiful? What did Ben care?

And I don't care either. I'll get her looking the best she can—because she deserves it. She needs all the reassurance she can get. She'll feel a lot more confident, a lot more comfortable about what we've just gone and done, if she can wipe that vile word out of her mental vocabulary.

He heard it again, cruel and ugly.

Grotesque.

Well, that word was going in the trash can. And staying there. He would never let her say it again.

CHAPTER EIGHT

'WINE for you?' Rico held the bottle of chilled white wine over Lizzy's glass.

'Um—er—thank you,' she replied awkwardly, and he proceeded to fill it up.

They were back at the table on the terrace again, but over the sea the sun was sinking in a glory of red and gold.

'Mummy, I'm really hungry,' Ben said plaintively.

'Food is coming very soon,' said Rico, pouring himself a glass of wine as well.

'What are we having for tea, Mummy?'

Rico smiled. 'Pasta, Ben. All good children in Italy eat pasta. Do you like pasta?'

'I *love* pasta,' Ben exclaimed.

'In Italy you can eat pasta every day,' said Rico.

He lifted his wine glass.

'To our first day here,' he said, looking at Ben and his mother. Ben lifted his glass of orange juice. 'Have we had a good day, everyone?' he asked around.

'Yes,' said Ben.

'Yes,' said his mother. 'It's been lovely.'

It had too, and Lizzy was grateful. It was strange. She hadn't expected it to be easy. And yet it had been. They'd done nothing except spend most of the day on the beach, coming back up to the terrace for lunch, and then, after much protesting from Ben, having a brief siesta. When Ben had surfaced they'd gone down to the beach again, returning only in late afternoon for Ben to have a quick swim in the pool, before showering and getting ready for supper.

The only awkward moment had been when Ben, splashing around in the warm shallow sea with his uncle, had called out 'Mummy, aren't you going to swim?'

Lizzy had shaken her head, the thought of stripping off to a bathing costume making her cringe. It was bad enough being on a beach with a man whose honed, lean-muscled body, clad only in swimming trunks, made it impossible to let her eyes go anywhere near him.

'I'll swim another time,' she'd evaded, and gone doggedly back to her book.

Other than that it had been an extraordinarily easy day. Now, sitting watching the sun set while they shared in a nursery tea, she realised she was feeling far more relaxed than she'd thought possible. She took a sip of her chilled wine.

'Is the wine to your liking?' Ben's uncle asked.

'Um—yes, it's lovely. I—er—I don't really know anything about wine,' she answered.

'You will learn with practice.' He smiled at her. 'And another thing you will learn with practice,' he went on, taking his own mouthful of wine, 'is to call me by name.'

Lizzy stared. She couldn't do that. The whole thing about addressing him had been so awkward that she simply hadn't done it. She couldn't address him as 'Highness', and she couldn't address him as 'Prince Enrico', or even 'Prince Rico'. And she certainly couldn't address him as simply Rico.

'And I must do the same,' he continued. 'So—' He took a breath. 'Lizzy. There, I've said it. Now it's your turn.'

'I can't,' said Lizzy. Embarrassment flushed through her.

'Have some more wine—then try,' he advised.

She took another mouthful, and swallowed hard.

'Rico,' she mumbled. She couldn't quite look at him.

'*Bene,*' he said softly. 'You see—all things are possible.' For a moment he held her eyes approvingly, then, with a change of tone, he spoke again. 'Ah, supper arrives.'

'Hurrah,' said Ben.

The following days were spent very largely as the first one had been. Rico made it so quite deliberately. He was giving her the time she needed—a breathing space.

He needed one too, he knew. They all did. He'd said as much to her the next day.

'We'll take this a day at a time, like I said,' he'd told her. 'We won't think about the outside world, we won't think about anything. We'll just accept the present and relax. Get used to things—get to know each other.'

It was ironic, he realised—all his life there had been a distance between himself and the world. There had had to be. And that meant, he acknowledged, that there were very few people that he ever truly let down his guard with. Jean-Paul was one, and there were a few others. Sportsmen, mostly, to whom his birth was a complete irrelevance, and all that counted was skill and dedication.

But never women—even in the superficial intimacies of the bed.

He'd bedded a lot in his time. Taken his pick, enjoying them physically. Making sure they enjoyed him, too.

But nothing more. Safety in numbers, he'd told Luca, and it had been true.

His mouth twisted. Had he proposed marriage, any of the women he'd bedded would have, in his brother's cruel words, bitten his hand off to accept. The prospect of becoming the glittering Principessa Enrico Ceraldi would have been irresistible to them.

Yet the woman he'd actually married had been horrified at the prospect.

He knew it was because of the outward disparities between

them, which she was so hung up about. Yet her attitude towards him had, he realised slowly, had another effect on him as well.

It had made him feel safe with her.

Because it made her like no other woman he knew.

It was a strange realisation, seeping through him.

All she wants from me is protection for Ben—that's all. She wants nothing else—nothing from me.

A thought came to him—another strange, new realisation.

I don't have to be on my guard with her. I don't have to keep her at a distance. Because she doesn't want anything from me—

A sense of release came over him, as if for the first time in his life, he felt—free.

Lizzy sat in the shade of the blue and white striped awning and watched Ben and his uncle play waterpolo in the pool. Ben was shrieking with pleasure. Her heart warmed. He was just so happy—every day had been a delight for him.

And for her?

It was so strange. How could it be that, despite the huge emotional upheaval she'd gone through since that fateful evening when her world had been turned upside down and she had discovered the truth about Ben's parentage, she could now be feeling so…carefree?

So relaxed.

And yet she was.

It had seemed impossible at the outset of their panicked arrival here. The enormity of what had happened, what she had done, had been overwhelming, and yet here, in this tranquil, beautiful place—so far from the rest of the world, it seemed—she had found a peace of mind she had never thought to find.

Her eyes went to the man playing with her son, and she felt gratitude welling through her—and wonder.

He was being so kind to her. And not just because of Ben.

He had gone out of his way to be endlessly kind and patient to her, for her own sake.

It was a world away from his image as the Playboy Prince. There's more to him than that. Much more, she thought fiercely.

She had misjudged him, she knew, seeing only the image, not the man beneath. He was a man who had defied his father, his sovereign, to defend and protect her and Ben. A man who had unhesitatingly married himself to the very last woman in the world he'd ever have chosen for a wife for the sake of a small child.

A child he really seemed to love.

She felt her heart warm as she watched Rico haul himself out of the pool. His lean body glittered with diamonds in the sun as he leant down, let Ben clutch his arm with his hands, and with effortless strength lifted him clear out of the water.

'Again!' shouted Ben, and jumped back in the water.

Rico repeated the process, swinging him high into the air with a laughing grin before lowering him gently to the paving beside the pool.

Ben rushed up to Lizzy.

'I scored *five* goals,' he exclaimed.

'Did you? How fantastic.' She smiled.

'Why don't you come in the water, Mummy?'

'Because she needs a nice new swimming costume, Ben. And lots of new clothes, like you've already had. Clothes for a princess.'

Rico had come up behind him.

Ben tilted his head to one side. 'Is Mummy a princess, then?'

'Yes,' said Rico casually, padding himself dry with a towel. 'When I married her she became a princess.'

'Has she got a crown?' Ben asked interestedly. He had a strong mental association between royalty and crowns.

'She can have a tiara. For when she goes to a ball.'

Ben's eyes lit up.

'Like Cinderella?'

'Exactly like Cinderella,' said Rico.

His eyes went to Lizzy's face, and then shadowed. There was a look in her eyes he did not want there, but he knew why it was.

Lizzy looked away. If there was any role in Cinderella she was ideally cast for, it was not the heroine. It was as an ugly sister.

It was Maria—Maria who had been Cinderella—swept off her feet by Prince Charming. But the coach had crashed.

Rico saw her look away. Read her thought. His mouth pressed tight. It was time to get this sorted. Time to put that cruel word in the trash once and for all.

She was comfortable with him now, he knew—and he with her. But that harsh word still remained between them like a poison. A poison that needed to be drawn.

And there was no point delaying it any longer. It was time, more than time, to do something about it.

It proved very easy to arrange. The shopping complex by the marina was designed to cater to the needs of those who stayed at Capo D'Angeli. And those needs included the overwhelming demand to attend to their appearance—clothes, hair, beauty treatments, manicures; whatever was required was available.

He would book the lot, and let them loose on her.

The following day, at breakfast, he made his announcement.

'I will look after Ben today. You will be too busy.'

Lizzy stared. 'Busy?' she asked. Apprehension filled her.

Rico only smiled cryptically. 'Very busy,' he said.

Within the hour, she found out just how busy.

Lizzy had her eyes shut. Over her head, it sounded as if the army of people who had invaded her bedroom were having a heated argument. They weren't, she knew—they were just discussing her. But in a very Italianate manner they were doing so vehemently, with many loud exclamations. She could understand why. They had been given an impossible brief—to spin straw into gold.

Make a silk purse out of a sow's ear.

Mortification filled her.

She'd known this moment must come. Known that, however desperate the circumstances of her sudden marriage to Rico had been, they could not hide here at the villa for ever. At some point they would have to emerge. Face the world.

The prospect appalled her.

She could wear all the designer clothes in the world, but it would still be her underneath. Nothing could change that. Maria had looked a knock-out even in rags, because she'd had a face, a body, that was a knock-out.

Guilt knifed through her. Guilt and grief. Oh, God, it should be Maria here, in this beautiful Italian villa, having her honeymoon with her golden prince. Looking forward blissfully to their happy-ever-after. Their own personal fairytale.

Her hands twisted in her lap. Grief and guilt twisted together.

And not just guilt for her sister.

I've got to go through with this. I've got to bear it. It doesn't matter how humiliating it is, how mortifying. I have to let them do what they can. Do the best they can.

But it wasn't for her. It was for the man who had married her to keep Ben safe, the man whose reward was to be saddled with a wife in a marriage that all the world would call by the only word that suited it—*grotesque.*

A man like Prince Rico, the Playboy Prince, accustomed to the most beautiful women in the world falling for him—now married to a woman like her.

She opened her eyes. The arguing stopped instantly. She looked around at the sea of faces, all watching her expectantly.

She took a deep breath.

'Please,' she said, 'just do the best you can.'

Then she shut her eyes again—and kept them shut.

'We need another tower,' Ben instructed.

Rico considered the masterwork on the terrace table. Then nodded.

'You're right,' he said. 'I'll fit one inside this corner. How's the painting coming along?'

'Good,' said Ben. He was industriously washing stone-grey paint across the expanse of large cardboard box that had been transformed into a fort to house an army of brightly coloured plastic knights in armour which had, to Ben's ecstasy, been ordered off the internet to be delivered by courier the following morning. Ben's impatience for their arrival had been such that on their return to the terrace from the beach and the pool Rico had been driven to suggest they make a fort for the knights to live in when they arrived. Its construction also helped to divert Ben from the fact he had not seen his mother all day.

Anxiety nagged at Rico.

Was she going to be all right? It was late afternoon already, but he knew that beauty treatments took for ever, and the fact that she had been incarcerated all day did not surprise him. But how was she coping with it all?

Well, it couldn't be much longer, surely?

He reached for the scissors and began the tricky business of cutting cardboard for the requisite tower. He needed diverting as well.

'Is Mummy *still* trying on new clothes?' Ben demanded

'It takes ladies a long time,' said Rico. 'And to do their hair and things.'

'It doesn't take Mummy long,' Ben countered. 'She's always very quick.'

'Now that she's got to be a princess it will need to take longer,' Rico answered.

Ben stared down the long terrace towards where the bedrooms opened on to it. Then, suddenly, his expression changed.

'Mummy.'

He dropped the paintbrush and pushed his chair back.

Rico looked up.

And froze.

* * *

Ben was hurtling along the terrace towards her as Lizzy stepped gingerly out through the French windows from her bedroom.

'Mummy—Mummy, you've been ages! We're making a fort, Uncle Rico and me. For the soldiers—they are knights in armour. They're coming tomorrow, in a special van, and they are a present for being good. And we're making a fort for them. Come and see—come and see.'

He seized her hand and started to pull her along. She tottered momentarily, uncertain of her balance on the sandals that, although low-heeled, seemed to consist of nothing but two minute strips of leather.

'Come on, Mummy,' Ben said, impatient at her slowness.

But the last thing on earth she wanted was to go where he was leading her.

Towards the terrace table, towards the man who sat there, quite, quite motionless.

There was no expression on his face.

Her heart started to slump heavily in her chest cavity, hollowing out a space around it. She felt sick.

Sick with dismay.

Oh, God—all that work, all that time, and it's a disaster—I can see it in his face. It's awful, awful.

It had taken so *long*—hours and hours. And so much had been done to her. All over. There had been so much chattering, and agitation, and volatility, that she had just let them get on with it. The treatments had gone on and on, one after another. Spreading stuff on her body, then wiping it off again, and on her face several more times. Then she'd had her hair washed, and more stuff had been put on it, and left in, then rinsed out, and different stuff put on. And in the meantime the tweezers had come out, and nail files and buffers and varnish and hot wax, and yet more body wraps and creams. She had had to eat lunch, served in her room, with her face and hair covered in gunk and her body swathed in some kind of thin gown. And while she'd eaten yet another one of the army of people in her room had held up one garment after another, off a trio of racks that had been wheeled in—so many garments that she'd simply lost count.

'Please,' she had murmured faintly, 'whatever you think best.'

And finally the last of the wraps had come off, and the rollers had come out of her hair, and it had been blow-dried—though heaven knew what rollers and blow-drying would do for her hopelessly frizzy hair. Then yet another beautician had gone to work on her, with a vast amount of make-up, before, at the very last, she had been lifted to her feet and one outfit after another had been whisked on to her, commented on by all in the room, then replaced with another one and the process repeated.

Until one had been left on her, her hair and make-up had been retouched one last time, and she had been gently but insistently guided towards the French windows.

She had no idea what she looked like. She could see she had nail varnish on—a soft coral-apricot colour—and her hands felt smooth and soft. Her hair felt different—lighter somehow. As if it were lifting as she walked instead of hanging in a heavy clump as it normally did. As for her clothes—she could see she was wearing a cinnamon-coloured dress, with a close-fitting bodice and cap sleeves, a narrow belt around the waist and a skirt that floated like silk around her legs.

But she hadn't seen a reflection of herself. No one had asked her whether she wanted to see in a mirror, and she had been too cowardly to want to anyway. Deferring the evil moment.

But now it had arrived, and she wanted to die.

Oh, God—what had been the point of it all?

She must look ridiculous, absurd—dressed up like this, done up to the nines. All such fine feathers could do was show just how awful she was underneath.

Hot, hopeless embarrassment flooded through her. Why had

she let them do this to her? She should have just stayed as she was—accepted what she was.

The ugly sister. Who, even when she was dressed up for the ball in gorgeous clothes, was still the ugly sister.

At her side, Ben was chattering away as she walked slowly, mortifyingly forward—towards the figure seated, motionless, under the parasol at the terrace table.

Her eyes went to him, full of dread, and as she looked at him she felt her stomach give its familiar hopeless clench.

He was wearing shorts, and a white T-shirt that strained across his torso, and he was watching her approach with absolutely no expression on his face whatsoever.

She tore her gaze away from him as she felt the hot, horrible heat of exposure rise in her. She wanted to turn and run, to bolt back to the safety of her bedroom, hide there for ever and never come out again…

She reached the table.

Say something. Anything.

She swallowed hard.

'Oh, Ben—that's a wonderful fort.' Her voice sounded high-pitched and false. And coming from a hundred miles away.

'Me and Tio Rico made it. It's got two towers, and a bridge that lifts right up, and look, Mummy, it's got a porcully that goes up and down. Tio Rico made it work. Look, I'll show you, Mummy—'

She forced herself to look as Ben tugged on the string that operated the portcullis.

'That's really good,' she said in a strangulated voice.

I've got to look at him. I must.

It was the hardest thing in the world to do, but she did it. She turned her head so that she was looking straight at him. Looking straight at that totally expressionless face.

'It's a brilliant fort,' she said to him weakly.

He answered in Italian.

'Non credo—'

She swallowed, her stomach hollowing. What didn't he believe? That so much time and effort expended on her should be so wasted?

The sickness in her stomach churned hideously.

Ben was still talking, and she tried to listen, but it was impossible. Something about where all his new knights would go—which ones would be inside the castle, and which would be attacking it. His little voice went in and out.

And opposite her, still motionless, Prince Rico of San Lucenzo just looked at her, without a shred of expression on his face.

He was in shock, he realised. Shock so profound that he was still fighting to get his brain around what his eyes were telling him.

It wasn't possible, what he was seeing. It just wasn't.

It could not be the same woman. It just couldn't.

It was impossible. Physically impossible.

She absolutely, totally, completely was *not* the woman he had last seen.

Dio—where had she *come* from? That body. That fantastic, gorgeous, *lush* body. An absolutely perfect *bella figura*. With a cinched-in waist that curved out to a pair of perfectly rounded hips, and up…he swallowed…up to a pair of breasts so ripe, so luscious, so beautifully moulded by the material swelling over them that he just wanted to…he just wanted to…

He felt his body react. He couldn't stop it. It was there—urgent, irrepressible, unstoppable. A complete, total insistence on letting him know just *exactly* what it felt about what his eyes were seeing.

With an effort he did not know he was capable of, he forced his eyes upward. But it did him no good.

The reaction was exactly the same.

The rest of her went with the figure.

It was the hair—what the *hell* had happened to her hair? The frizz had simply gone. As if it had never existed. In its place, tinted to a rich chestnut, was a smooth, glossy mane that waved

back from her face, pouring down over her shoulders in a luxu-
riant swathe.

As for her face—

How had he not seen it? Shock punched through him again.
Delicately arched eyebrows over endlessly deep, long-lashed,
luminous eyes, cheekbones that arced to a perfect nose, that de-
scended to a mouth…

He swallowed silently.

A mouth that was rich, and lush, and… *Dio*, so inviting…

Someone was talking. Tugging at his arm.

'Tio Rico. You're not listening. Is it time for tea now?
Mummy's come out at last and I'm *hungry*,' he finished
plaintively.

Where he found the strength of mind he didn't know. But
somehow he dragged his eyes to Ben.

'Yeah—sure, right. You want to eat? OK. That's fine.' He
said some more in Italian, just as incoherent.

*What the hell was going on? Had the universe just stopped
and restarted in a different dimension? A dimension where impossible things were totally normal?*

She was saying something. Her voice was more high-pitched
than usual, and she was trying to sound relaxed and casual, and
failing completely.

'Has Ben been OK today? I'm sorry I…er…I took so
long. I…er…'

Her voice trailed off.

He was staring at her again. He couldn't take his eyes from
her. It was impossible.

For a moment Lizzy just went on standing there, while the
expressionless face in front of her just looked blankly at her.

Then suddenly, totally, she couldn't cope. Just couldn't. She
felt as if a stone had been punched into her solar plexus. It was
almost a physical pain. She turned on her spindly heels and
plunged off. She didn't know where. Just anywhere. Anywhere.

She didn't know where she was going. The terrace ended in

steps, down to the swimming pool level, and she just clattered down them, almost tripping in her desperation, past the glittering azure pool, to plunge on to the narrow stepped path that wound its way down to the sea between the vegetation and the pines. Her heart was pounding, and she could feel a sick, horrible flush in her cheeks.

She wanted to die.

Why had she let them do it? She should have known it was hopeless, useless, pointless. Hot, horrible mortification scorched through her.

I shouldn't have tried—I shouldn't have tried to make myself look better. Normal. Trying and failing is even worse than just accepting what I am—ugly, ugly, ugly...

She could hear footsteps hurrying behind her, heavy and pounding, and her name being called. She hurried faster, her heel catching in her haste, so that she had to lurch and clutch at the railing beside the pathway before trying to go on.

But her arm was being caught, held.

'Stop. What is it? What's wrong?'

She tensed in every muscle, trying to tear her arm away. His fingers pressed like steel into her bare flesh.

'Go away.'

The words burst from her. She couldn't stop them. Her head whipped round.

'Go away. Leave me alone. *Leave me alone!*'

There was shock and bewilderment in his face.

'What's happened? What's wrong?'

'What do you mean, what's wrong? Everything's wrong. *Everything,*' she gasped.

She just stood there, frozen and immobile, tugging hopelessly away from him, while he held her, feet planted on the step above, towering over her.

He was so close. Far too close. She tried to tug back again, but it was hopeless, useless. Just as everything was hopeless, useless.

For a moment he said nothing—just looked at her. A look

of complete incomprehension filled his face. Then, as he looked, the expression of shock and bewilderment began to change. She saw it happening, saw it and did not believe it.

It was something in his eyes. Something that seemed slowly to be dissolving. Dissolving not just in his eyes, but dissolving *her*. Turning her liquid, like wax left on a surface that was very slowly heating up.

The way her skin was heating. Flushing with a low, soft heat that seemed to be carried by the low, soft pulse of her blood that was creaming, like liquid sugar, like honey, through her veins.

She felt his grip on her change. Not so much halting her as...holding her. Holding her in position. Holding her just where he wanted her to be. Wanted her to be because...because...

The world had stopped moving. Everything had stopped moving. She was just there, immobile, held. And he was looking down into her face—and the expression in his eyes simply stayed the breath in her throat.

She gazed back up at him. What had happened, she didn't know. Reality wasn't there any more.

And yet it had never seemed more vivid.

'Don't look at me like that,' he said, in that low, soft voice that was curling the toes of her feet, sending liquid waves down her spine in long, honeyed undulations. 'Don't look at me like that here, now. Because if you go on looking at me like that, I'll—'

'Mum-my! *Mum-my.*'

They pulled apart, jerking away from each other. It was like surfacing from a deep, drowning sea.

'He's all right. I told him not to move.' Rico's voice sounded staccato, abstracted. He took a rapid, restoring breath.

'Mummy. Tio Rico.'

Ben's insistent call came again. Lizzy could hear alarm in it.

'I'm coming, Ben,' she called up. Her voice was shaky.

'Me too,' echoed Rico. His voice was not steady either.

He cast another look at her, then pulled his gaze away. It wasn't safe to look at her. Not here, not now.

Later…later he would look.

More than look—

Suddenly, out of nowhere, a sense of exultation crashed through him.

With light, lithe steps, he led the way up to the terrace.

Emotion was surging through Rico. Strong, overwhelming and consuming. The universe might have turned itself upside down, but right now he didn't care. How it had happened was irrelevant. Completely irrelevant. It had happened, and that was all that he was registering.

Adrenaline pumped through him. More than adrenaline. Exhilaration. Something quite incredibly amazing had happened, and he didn't want explanations—he just wanted to…to go with it.

'Here we are, Ben,' he announced as he gained the pool terrace, and he waved his hand at the little figure perched obediently on the upper level, straining his eyes downwards.

'Where is Mummy?' Ben demanded.

'Here—' said Lizzy, hurrying up the steps as fast as she could in her flimsy sandals. Her heart was racing.

It had nothing to do with her rapid ascent.

As she gained the terrace Ben stared at her, paying attention to her for the first time, instead of to his new fort.

'Is that your new dress?' he asked.

She swallowed, nodded.

He tilted his head sideways, inspecting her. Then he frowned.

'You look all pretty. Like in a magazine. But you don't look like Mummy.' He frowned, confused and bewildered.

Rico put an arm around his nephew's shoulder. He knew just how Ben was feeling.

'She's the new-look Mummy. And you're right Ben.' His voice changed. 'She does look pretty. In fact she looks…' He paused, and held her eyes. 'Breathtaking,' he finished softly. 'Quite, quite breathtaking.'

For a long, endless moment, he held her eyes.

He saw her eyes flare—uncertain briefly—and then, suddenly, it had gone again.

'It's true,' he said quietly to her. 'Quite true. I can't believe…I can't believe that all this was there, all along. Just…hidden.' He paused, and then, in a low, clear voice, said, 'And you are never—do you understand me?—*never* going to hide it again.'

For one last, lingering moment he looked at her. Sending his message loud and clear.

Then, abruptly, he turned his head.

'Right, then, Ben. Time for tea.'

CHAPTER NINE

SHE was moving in a place that was completely dissociated from what she was doing. What she was actually doing was pouring out a cup of perfectly brewed Assam tea from a silver teapot, while Ben was industriously, if inexpertly, coiling spaghetti around his fork. The DIY fort had been cleared away for the moment, and the westering sun was bathing the terrace in rich, deep golden glow.

The same glow was inside her, suffused through her, so that it seemed she was part of the warm golden light all around her. It dazed her, bemused her—and she gave herself to it because she couldn't do anything else.

As she sipped at her hot, fragrant tea her eyes slipped of their own accord to the man sitting opposite her. He lounged back, his pose so relaxed that he was like a young, lithe leopard taking its ease, taking indolent mouthfuls of espresso coffee every now and then, one arm spread out across his chair-back, one long leg casually crossed over a lean, bare thigh. He was chatting to Ben, answering the child's questions with lazy good humour, but his eyes would flicker over her as he chatted, sending tiny little shots of electricity quivering through her.

Her glow deepened.

What was happening was beyond her—completely and absolutely beyond her—and she didn't care. She didn't want to question, or analyse, or examine or understand. She just wanted to give herself to this wonderful, dazed bemusement that had taken her over, filling her with this rich, warm glow that reached through every cell of her body.

After Ben had eaten his tea, they played cards. A noisy, fast game that involved a lot of slapping down of cards and crows of triumph from both Ben and Rico. Yet even in the midst of the game Rico could still find time to glance at her, still feel the echoes of that incredible shock wave that had slammed through him as she'd approached him along the terrace, her transformation so incredible he could not, even now, fully believe it.

And yet it was there in front of him, the evidence of his own eyes. A miracle.

Her hair by itself was a miracle. The frizz had simply vanished—he hadn't known it was possible, and yet clearly it was. Her skin was clear and glowing, her make-up bringing to life features which he'd thought nondescript and unremarkable.

And now his eyes kept going back to her, time and time again.

He wanted her. He knew it, and he had no intention of denying it.

It was impossible to do so. His body had recognised it in the first moments of seeing her walk towards him, displaying that fantastic lush figure which had so incredibly been there all along—invisible under the shapeless, baggy clothes she'd worn.

How the hell had she kept it hidden?

He still couldn't get his head round it. To have such a full, lush body as that, and yet to hide it.

Well, there was no hiding it now. None at all. Never, ever again would she ever hide herself.

Especially not from him.

He felt his body react again, and had to struggle to subdue it.

He must not rush this. Dared not. She was walking a knife-edge, still in a state of shock, of disbelief about herself.

I've got to take this slowly. Very slowly.

Let her get used to it. Let her come to believe it. Take her slowly, so slowly, every step of the way.

His eyes rested on her yet again, while Ben dealt out another round, his little voice counting the cards diligently as he set them down in three piles.

He could see her awareness of him even as she oversaw Ben's dealing. Saw it in the swift, covert glance, the slight tremor of her hand as she picked up her cards.

Lizzy could see him looking at her, see it and feel it. It was tangible, like the lightest caress on her skin.

She felt her heart skip a beat, skitter inside her...

What's happening—what's happening to me?

It was a stupid, idiotic question to ask. She knew exactly what was happening to her. And she couldn't stop it. Could no more stop it than she could have stopped a whirlpool sucking her down.

She was responding to the core-deep, devastating sexuality of the man she had married to keep Ben safe with her. And how could she help it?

Ever since she had first set eyes on him, that terrible traumatic night in Cornwall, she had responded to him. She had crushed it down, embarrassed by it, knowing that she must never show the slightest sign of her response because for someone like her to do so would be...*grotesque*.

It had been easy enough to do. To him, she had simply not existed as a female. Nor did she to any man, she knew. So, although her instinctive reaction to him had been embarrassing and pointless, she had also known that it really hadn't mattered at all—it had been completely irrelevant.

All that had mattered had been Ben.

And these last few days, when he had visibly gone out of his way to try and make her feel more at ease with what had so traumatically happened to her, when he'd been kind, and nice, and nothing like the Playboy Prince of his reputation, it had still not mattered. More than not mattered.

It had allowed her to start to relax around him. Start to feel at ease around him. Start to see him not as a prince, nor as a man—but as a person.

They had talked—nothing special, nothing earth-shatter-
ing, just easy conversation. About Ben, yes, but about other
things too, over meals, and on the beach, and while Ben was
playing, absorbed, with his trains and all the other toys that
had been delivered to the villa or which he'd discovered in
the playroom.

She wasn't sure what they'd talked about—nothing much came
to mind—but she knew was that it hadn't been a strain, an effort.

It had been…friendly.

Easygoing, casual, relaxed.

But now—now it felt as if tiny bubbles were fizzing through
her veins. Effervescing inside her.

Every time he glanced at her.

What's happening to me?

But she knew. She knew.

'Goodnight, darling, sleep tight.'

Lizzy bent over to drop a kiss on Ben's cheek. He was asleep
already, she could see. On the other side of the bed, Rico
reached out and ruffled his hair gently.

He had insisted on giving Ben his bath that night.

'We don't want Mummy's new dress getting wet, do we?'
he'd said.

Instead, he had been the one to get wet. Lizzy could see
where the damp T-shirt clung to his torso. She averted her eyes,
but not before Rico had spotted her doing so.

There was a decided glint in his eye as he spoke.

'I'll go and get myself cleaned up, then join you for
dinner, OK?'

He had given instructions to the chef for a proper dinner that
night. Whatever the results of Lizzy's makeover would prove,
he intended to make the evening special for her.

And it would be special indeed. Another wave of disbelief
went over him. They had been doing so regularly, every time
he looked at her.

It was incredible, just incredible.

He frowned momentarily.

Had she actually looked at herself yet? Surely she must have? And yet that initial reaction, when she'd run from him, blurting that it had all been a disaster, argued that she surely could not have seen the transformation.

He came around the foot of the bed.

'You may need some kind of wrap,' he told her. 'The nights can still be a little chilly. Let's see what you've got.'

He opened the closet door and went in. All her new clothes hung in serried ranks, swathed in plastic protectors. He glanced at them with approval. There was a lot here, and that was good. He wanted her to have as many beautiful outfits as possible. This was just the start.

She had followed him in, just as he'd intended.

'Where would you store a wrap?' he asked.

But Lizzy didn't answer him. Could not.

The whole rear wall of the closet was a mirror, and standing in the mirror, looking back at her, was someone she had never seen before in her life.

Rico straightened and looked first at the woman in the mirror, then at the woman staring at her.

He let her look. Let the look of dazed incomprehension fill her face.

Then he spoke.

'It's you. The you that you really are. The you that was hiding all this time.'

His voice was steady, level—merely stating a fact. A fact he would no longer let her deny. Conceal.

Her eyes were wide, huge.

'It can't be me. It can't.'

Her voice was faint.

He came and stood behind her.

'Oh, it's you, all right.'

Lightly, oh so lightly, he rested his hands on her shoulders.

Her skin was like satin. He felt her tremble at his touch, but she did not move. She went on staring.

'How did they do it?' she asked faintly.

He gave a smile. 'They had good material to work with.'

She lifted her hand to her hair, then dropped it wonderingly.

'But my hair—all that frizz—'

'They fixed it. There must be chemicals they use that change the hair somehow. After that, all they had to do was...do you up.' His voice softened. 'It was always there, Lizzy. Always. And now it always will be.'

He dropped his hands away.

He didn't want to. He wanted to glide them down her arms, turn her around, lower his mouth to hers and...

But he knew he must not. Not now, not here.

Not yet.

Instead, he stepped back.

'Do you think they'd have put wraps in a drawer?' he asked. 'Let's have a look.'

Rico reached out his arm and closed his hand around the neck of the champagne bottle, drawing it up out of its bucket of ice and refilling their glasses.

They were sitting at the table on the terrace, but it had been transformed from its daytime appearance, when it was usually covered with Ben's toys and books. The parasol had disappeared, and a pristine white tablecloth had been draped crisply, laden down with silver and crystal. A beautiful floral arrangement graced the centre, and the flames of long candles in silver candlesticks flickered in the night air. Above, the stars glittered in the black velvet sky. Out to sea, the lights from fisher boats glimmered in the dark. All around, cicadas kept their soft chorus, and the scent of flowers wafted softly.

The meal had done justice to the setting. Exquisitely prepared and presented, each delicacy had been too tempting to resist. And Lizzy had not resisted—nor did she resist a second glass of the light, foaming liquid that glinted in the candlelight in its tall, elegant flute.

'To you,' said Rico, and raised his glass. 'To the new you. The real you.'

The staff had gone, leaving them to coffee, tiny crisp *biscotti*, and the rest of the champagne. It was a rare vintage, and Rico savoured it.

It was not all that he was savouring.

He took a mouthful, appreciating the dry biscuit of the champagne, and leant back. His eyes rested on the woman opposite.

She had found a wrap, a soft swathe in a subtle mix of hues that blended and complemented the cinnamon of her dress. She had draped it around her shoulders, one end scooped across her throat. It did not quite conceal the rich swell of her breasts in the beautifully cut bodice.

No, he must not let his eyes drift there. He wanted to—he badly wanted to—but he knew he must not. She could not cope with that. Not yet. He must take it slowly.

Savour it.

He took another mouthful of champagne, savouring that too.

'To you,' he said again. 'To the new, beautiful Elisabetta.'

His voice was liquid over the syllables. Then, abruptly, his brows drew together.

'How did anyone think to call you Lizzy?' He said the short form of her name disparagingly.

Lizzy's eyes flickered uncertainly. 'I've always been Lizzy,' she said.

'And yet you were also always Elizabeth—Elisabetta.' There was a sudden edge in Rico's voice, which softened as he repeated the Italian form of her name. Then his brows drew together again, questioningly, frowningly. 'Was it your sister who did it to you?'

The edge was back in his voice.

'Did what?' Again her eyes flickered uncertainly.

'Was it your sister who turned you into Lizzy?'

'I don't understand,' she answered, puzzled and uncertain.

'I've always been called Lizzy. Frizzy-Lizzy, because of my hair. Or Busy-Lizzy, usually.'

'Did she keep you busy, waiting on her hand and foot?' His voice was dry.

'Maria?' Lizzy's brow furrowed, confused 'Maria was the best sister anyone could ever have.' She felt her throat tighten dangerously. 'She was truly a golden girl. Everyone loved her. She was so beautiful. She was tall, and slender, and she had long, long legs, and her hair was like honey, and hung straight to her waist, and she had beautiful blue eyes, and even when she was at school the boys were all over her, and when she became a model she was even more beautiful, and no wonder a prince fell for her—' She halted abruptly.

Rico picked his words carefully.

'Maria was pretty—very pretty. But she was...' He paused. Bimbo, Luca had called her. Cruel and callous. And yet Ben's natural mother had, indeed, possessed the kind of eye-candy looks that gave rise to that harsh dismissal.

'Hers is not the only kind of beauty,' he said.

But if Maria's sister had grown up being told that only candyfloss blondeness was acceptable, that the kind of ultra-slim figure that suited models was the only ticket in town, then no wonder she'd never tried to make anything of the looks she had. No wonder she'd settled for being Busy-Lizzy, living in the shadow of her sister.

'So who called you Busy-Lizzy?' The edge was back again.

'That was Maria,' she said with a half-laugh, making herself do so. 'But she didn't mean it in a bad way. She used to say it to me in exasperation. Because I never—'

She halted, reaching for her glass of champagne and taking a deliberate sip to cover her silence.

'Never what?' probed Rico.

What had happened to her? What had made her see herself as ugly? He had thought it might be her sister, and yet she denied it. So what, then?

He wanted to know. Wanted to find out what had been done to her, and by whom.

'Because you never what?' he prompted again.

He wanted answers. Wanted to understand. So that the poison in her would come out once and for all. Never to return.

'I never stopped,' she answered.

'Stopped what?'

'Being busy, I suppose. Being useful.'

'Who to?' he asked in a low voice.

He saw her fingers tighten around the stem of her flute.

'Maria. My parents.'

'Why did they need you to be useful?'

Her eyes wouldn't meet his.

'Because—' she stopped.

'Because?' he prompted. Quietly, insistently.

Her fingers pressed on the glass. He could see her fingers whiten where they gripped.

'Because it was all I was good for. I wasn't beautiful, like Maria, and she had all the brains, not me. She was all they needed—my parents.'

Her eyes had slid past him completely now. Staring ahead of her. Something was going wrong in her face; he could see it. She jerked the champagne glass to her lips and took a gulp. Then set it down, just as jerkily.

Then deliberately, almost angrily, her eyes snapped back to his.

'When Maria was born I ceased to have a function. Apart from that of handmaid. That was all I was good for. Looking after Maria. Helping Maria. Making way for Maria. Maria, Maria, Maria! Everything revolved around Maria. Me, I was just the spare wheel—surplus to requirements. Not wanted on voyage. Existing on sufferance—justified only if I looked after Maria, and even then barely. I wanted to hate her. But I couldn't. I couldn't hate her. No one could hate her. Because there was nothing to hate. There really wasn't. She really was a golden girl. Everyone loved her. No wonder my parents adored her.

They adored her so much they forgave her everything. Even becoming a model. There was only one thing they didn't forgive her for. Only one thing.' She stilled, then spoke again.

'Dying. That's what they could not forgive her for.'

She bowed her head, as if bowing beneath a weight.

'They couldn't live without her. So they didn't. They went into the garage, locked the doors, got into the car, and turned the engine on.'

For a moment there was silence. Complete silence. Rico felt cold ice through him.

'Your parents killed themselves?' His voice was hollow. This had not been in the dossier on Maria Mitchell.

'Once they knew she would never recover. That she would be a vegetable—in a coma until....'

She halted. Her face was stark, even in the candlelight.

'She was everything to them—their whole world. They had dedicated their lives to her. And she had gone. Left them. Left them to go modeling.' She swallowed again. 'Left them to go off with some man who had, so they thought, simply "got her into trouble"—and then she left them utterly. Left them all alone.'

Slowly, still with that cold draining through him, Rico spoke.

'But they had her baby—and you.'

She looked at him. Her eyes had no expression in them.

'The baby was a bastard—fatherless, an embarrassment, a disgrace. As for me, I was…an irrelevance. I didn't count,' she said. 'I was—unnecessary—to them.'

His eyes darkened. He felt the anger rising in him like a cold tide.

Unnecessary. The word had a grim, familiar sound.

He was unnecessary too. Had been all his life. He was the spare—surplus to requirements. To be put on a shelf and left there, just in case of emergencies. But with no other purpose then simply to pass the time, fritter his life away until and in case he should ever be needed, cease to be unnecessary.

He felt the anger lash through him again. But this time it was at himself. For having accepted his parents' verdict on him. Oh, he had resented the role he'd been born to, but he'd still accepted that that was all he was. The spare to Luca's heir.

Well, that wasn't true any longer.

Emotion swept through him. He looked at the woman sitting opposite him, who had been so horrifically *unnecessary* to her parents—but who was so necessary to the one human being to whom *he*, too, had proved necessary.

He reached across the table and took her hand. He spoke with a low intensity.

'But you're necessary now—necessary and…essential. You are Ben's happiness, and I…I am his safety. And together—' his hand tightened around hers, warm, and safe and protecting '—we'll take care of him, and love him.'

Gently he drew her to her feet. Emotion filled him as he led her down the terrace to where the French windows to her room stood slightly ajar. Inside, they stood by the bed, looking down at Ben's sleeping form.

Rico's arm went around her shoulder as they stood, gazing down at the one human being on the earth to whom they were absolutely and totally necessary.

United in that.

And more, Rico knew.

'Hang on to your hats,' Rico yelled

'I'm not wearing one,' Ben yelled back, against the revving of the engine.

'Just as well,' riposted Rico, and let the throttle out.

The boat roared off, sleek and powerful, carving a foaming wake through the still blue water.

Lizzy's arm tightened around Ben automatically, but Ben was oblivious of anything except the thrill of being in a speed-boat. Wind whipped at her hair, half blinding her, and she had to grip with all her might to the boat rail. The hull slapped and slammed against the water, bumping like a rollercoaster ride.

'Wheee!' yelled Ben, ecstatically.

Rico turned from the wheel and grinned.

His hair was blown off his face and he looked younger, carefree.

'Faster?' he asked.

'Yes, yes,' Ben cried.

'Here we go, then.'

He accelerated, and the boat picked up yet more speed. Exhilaration filled him. This might not be anything like the speed of a powerboat in a race, but it was still fast and furious.

When finally he slewed around in a great curve, and started heading back to land, he slackened the throttle and turned to his passengers.

'Was that fun?' he asked with a grin, his eyes dancing.

'Yes!' yelled Ben.

'You're a complete maniac,' said Lizzy.

His grin widened. 'No, just Italian.' He eased back on the throttle even more as they headed for land at a sedate pace. He patted the wheel. 'She's not bad, but she's no powerboat. They can get to speeds of over a hundred knots. Now, that's really moving. Still, we'll have some fun in this one, won't we?'

Annoyance flared in him. The boat he'd hired from the marina was ideal for cruising around, exploring the coastline. But that wasn't something they could do yet. He would be recognised, it was inevitable, and then the press would start buzzing with rumours and speculation about who he was with, and why. He didn't want that. He wanted his marriage officially announced from the palace. Not out of consideration for his father, who deserved none after his callous treatment of Ben and his mother, but for Lizzy's sake.

She'd had enough stress already. All her life, in fact. Thanks to her parents—and everything that had happened since to her.

But so far there had been nothing but silence from the palace. Well, he'd given his father time enough to climb down, to accept what he'd done—perhaps he should send him a reminder.

He'd get on to it today. Jean-Paul would oblige, he knew.

Smoothly, he brought the boat into shore, cut and trimmed the engine, and dropped anchor in the shallow water. Ben jumped out without prompting, landing with a splash to wade ashore. Lithely, Rico climbed over the side himself, then held out his arms to Lizzy. She got rather unsteadily to her feet.

'I'm sure I can manage,' she said.

He scooped her up, and she gave a gasp. He grinned down at her. She was soft in his arms. Soft and voluptuous. And in the couture beach shorts and short-sleeved matching azure top she looked fantastic. Her hair was windblown, but that only gave her a tousled, wanton look.

'I'm too heavy for you,' she gasped.

He laughed scornfully, wading ashore with her. To think he had thought that her baggy, shapeless clothes had meant she was overweight. There wasn't a kilo of flesh on her that wasn't in the right place.

'I can bench twice your weight,' he said confidently. He lowered her gently to the sand, steadying her with his hands. She looked amazing. Her bare arms were smooth and already beginning to tan, now that they were finally being exposed to the sun.

She was beginning to get used to the transformation, he could see. The look of bewildered disbelief was rarer now; she was accepting what had happened. She was out of the box her parents had locked her into—a coffin for her womanhood.

Well, that was a box she would never go back into. And soon her womanhood would blaze into the glory it deserved.

His expression changed. Patience, he was discovering, was a hard virtue.

'Tio Rico, I need a new sandcastle. Come and help—' Ben's piping treble pierced the air.

Rico was glad of the diversion.

He phoned Jean-Paul after lunch. 'How would you feel about an exclusive photo-shoot?' he asked him. 'Ready for the glossies...'

He would send the photos to the palace first. Remind his father that time was running out for him, that if he kept on stonewalling Rico would simply make the announcement of his marriage himself—and let the press go to town on why the palace had let that happen.

'Don't wait too long, Rico. Security at Capo d'Angeli might be tight, but even so—' His friend's voice held a warning. 'This is a story to kill for.'

'I hear you—so can you do the shoot tomorrow?'

'I'll be there. Would I miss the second scoop of a lifetime on you?' Jean-Paul laughed, and signed off.

Slowly, Rico slid his phone away. His eyes travelled down the terrace to the French windows, behind which Lizzy was attempting to make Ben yield to an afternoon siesta. His thoughts went to them.

Jean-Paul was coming tomorrow. To take photos of the happy couple—the happy family. A fairytale marriage that would set a glow over them all. A perfect ending to the tale—the Playboy Prince marrying the adoptive mother of his brother's child.

Who had turned out to be Cinderella indeed—not the ugly sister she had always cast herself as. A Cinderella whose transformation had taken him by storm…inflamed his senses.

Whom he longed to embrace…possess…

A troubled look entered his eyes.

Did he have the right to do it? He wanted her, badly. He wanted her because she was a beautiful, alluring woman and he was bowled over by her—because his body was telling him, every time he saw her, that she was a woman to desire. And he wanted her, too, he knew, for *her* sake—because she had made him feel free and because he had seen her turn into a swan. Yes, she had emerged from the box she'd been locked into, and he wanted to lead her out of it—lead her to where every woman should go.

But did he have the right to take her there?

She's my wife. What other woman in the world should I desire?

His expression shadowed. Became sombre.

Yes, she was his wife—but their marriage was not about them, it was about Ben. Everything about their marriage, including those fairytale photos tomorrow, would be about Ben. His safety—his future. Not theirs.

Why not about our future? Why not about us?

The words formed in his head, coming from the same place deep within him that told him that the woman he wanted so much now was his wife—a wife to desire…to possess…

He sat very still as he realised what he was thinking.

Feeling.

Wanting.

He had married her, promising her a marriage of convenience purely to protect Ben, to protect her. When that had been achieved, when it would not cause any scandal, then he would end the marriage. Set her free. Set himself free.

I don't want that—

The realisation seared through him. Burning its way through his brain.

And in its wake came another emotion. He did not know what it was. He knew only that he was yielding to it, that it was far, far too strong for him to do anything else but yield to it.

And tonight—tonight he would do just that.

Tonight he would make his marriage real.

Those photos tomorrow would be no fairytale.

CHAPTER TEN

QUIETLY, Lizzy slipped from her room out on to the terrace, carefully lifting the long rustling skirts of her gown.

Ben was asleep. Reluctantly, but finally succumbing. It was later than his usual bedtime, but then he'd been judging a fashion parade. He and Rico had sat on the bed while she'd tried on one after another of her outfits, to choose which ones to wear the following day.

Nerves clipped at her as she thought about it. A photo-shoot, Rico had said. His friend Jean-Paul, to whom he had entrusted the story of their marriage, would undertake it.

She was glad Rico had suggested trying the outfits first, even though it seemed odd to have finished with her in evening dress.

'I want a full-length portrait photo of you,' Rico had said.

Then, when he'd finally chosen which gown he thought would be best for such a photo, he'd told her to leave it on.

'It will get you used to the feel and fit,' he'd told her, before heading off to get changed himself, for dinner.

She'd complied, though the close-fitting strapless dusky-rose silk gown with its flowing skirts, gorgeous though it was, seemed to make her somewhat over-dressed for a seaside villa.

'Ah, there you are—'

Rico's voice made her head turn.

And then her breath caught, and stilled in her lungs.

He was strolling towards her in the soft light spilling out on to the terrace, and he was wearing evening dress himself.

He looked—

She swallowed.

Oh, dear God, he looks incredible.

The tailored hand-made tuxedo moulded his long, lithe form, and made her legs feel weak. His freshly washed hair feathered over his forehead, and as he approached she caught the faintest tang of aftershave from his newly-shaved jawline.

She gazed at him helplessly, incapable of tearing her eyes away from him.

He came up to her. His eyes were on her, but all she could see was him.

A half-smile played about his lips.

'Buona sera, Principessa,' he said softly, and lifted her hand with his, to raise it to his lips.

His mouth grazed at her knuckles, and she felt a thousand butterflies release inside her.

He tucked her hand over his arm, and she found herself clinging to it. Numbly, she let herself be glided along the terrace.

'We're dining indoors tonight. Some light rain is forecast.'

She glanced absently at the sky, which was clouding over from the west. Then he was leading her into the large, formal dining room where they'd never eaten before.

She could see, as she looked round, why he had decided for them to wear evening dress. Her eyes widened. She'd never been in here, and she was astonished at its opulence. The huge glass table was edged with a gold metallic border, and an ornate chandelier festooned with crystals shone above. There seemed to be mirrors everywhere, and more glass and gold all around.

'It's a little overdone,' said Rico wryly.

He led her to her place and saw her seated. Then he took his own place opposite her. Almost immediately came the soft pop of a champagne cork, and then one of the staff was filling her flute before performing a similar office for Rico.

He lifted the glass.

'To us,' he said softly, his long lashes sweeping down over his dark eyes, and yet again Lizzy felt the fluttering wings inside her taking flight.

The meal passed as if in a dream. The silent, swift staff placed dishes in front of her, then whisked them away unnoticed. One by one the array of glasses at her place were filled, and then removed. She must have eaten and drunk, she knew, and it must have been delicious. And yet food and drink were the last things on her mind.

Her eyes were held, entirely and only, by the man sitting opposite her.

She felt weak. Incapable of doing anything except drink him in. She must have talked, she must have said things, but her mind was a daze. Inside her veins, the wine creamed in her blood, infusing her with a strange wonder.

I just want to look at him.

Gaze and gaze.

She had never allowed herself to do so before. Had always dragged her eyes away from him. Never indulged herself. But tonight—tonight was different. She didn't know why, didn't question. Merely let herself do what she had wanted to do since the very first time she had ever set eyes on him, and felt the shock of her reaction go through her.

Then, it had been forbidden to her. Then, she had been someone who would never have been allowed to do what she was doing now.

But she wasn't that person any more. She had been transformed, enchanted, into someone quite, quite different.

Someone who could gaze at him to her heart's desire.

Because he was doing the same to her.

The butterflies swooped and soared. His eyes were holding hers, and she was breathless, completely breathless.

He was getting to his feet, standing up. Holding out his hand to her.

'Come.'

It was all he said.

All he had to say.

She stood up. She could feel the silk rustling around her. She gathered the skirts into her fingers, making her way around the table to him. The strapless bodice clung to her, her hair brushed over her bare shoulders, her naked back.

He led her out into the hallway to the interior of the house. Opened another door and ushered her inside.

It was a bedroom.

And it was not hers.

He caught her shoulders, and turned her to him.

For one long, endless moment Rico gazed down at her, into those wide eyes, gazing up at him as they had gazed all evening.

How he had waited this long he did not know.

She hadn't realised, he knew, that her looking at him like that had been a torment to him. That it had taken all his self-control not to push back his chair, stride around the table to her, lift her up and crush her to him.

But he had not done so. Not just because the staff had still been about their business, not just because the chef had produced a *tour de force* that evening and to abandon it halfway through would have been unthinkably inconsiderate. Not just because he had known that with the night to come both of them would require sustenance.

But because he had known that she needed time.

Time to give herself to what was happening to them.

Did she know how much he desired her? He suspected not. The ways of men were an unknown country to her.

A realisation came to him, plunging through him.

Will I be her first?

Emotion scythed through him, flaring in his eyes. .

'Elisabetta.' He spoke softly, so softly, letting his voice pour through the liquid syllables.

His hands curved around her bare shoulders. Her skin was warm to his touch. He rested his thumbs along the delicate bones that arched to her throat and let them smooth her minutely. He felt her tremble beneath his touch.

She was still gazing up at him, her eyes huge, and in them was a longing that was unconscious in its intensity. It jolted through him, tipping him over the edge.

He could resist her no longer.

Slowly, infinitely slowly, he lowered his mouth to hers.

She gave a soft, helpless sigh, her eyes fluttering shut.

He kissed her slowly, very slowly. It was a soft kiss, a caress of her lips with his, and he could feel them shape themselves to him uncertainly, exploringly.

His mouth glided over hers like silk on water.

He took his time, an infinity of time.

This must be perfect for her—perfect.

He mustn't rush this, must take it at her pace, take her with him slowly, exquisitely, on the journey.

His mouth left hers, left her lips parted as his moved on, across the line of her jaw, to the hollow beneath her ear, gliding like silk, like gossamer, to where with the lightest of touches he caressed the outline of her earlobe.

One hand had slid around the nape of her neck, fingers teasing at the fine tendrils of her hair, while his other hand spanned the arch of her throat.

He felt the low, soft gasp vibrating through his fingers, and then his mouth was on hers again, teasing and caressing, until, with a sigh, she opened to him.

His body surged at the sheer sensuality of it as his tongue glided within. He felt her still, as if with shock, and then, as he intensified his kiss, he felt that moment come again as she yielded to his desire.

His hand swept down from the nape of her neck, along the naked length of her back. His fingers sought the fastening of her dress and, with a skill honed with practice over many years, he released the hook, and slowly, very slowly, slid down the zip.

He felt the bodice loosening against his torso and his hand at her throat moved downwards.

He wanted... He wanted...

Dio, but she was exquisite. Full, and soft—and yet as he cupped the silken mound he felt it ripen at his touch. Against his palm, her nipple flowered.

He felt his body surge again, insistent and demanding. Slowly, sensuously, he palmed her fullness.

She seemed to gasp in her throat, and arched her back, pressing herself against him.

It was all he needed. Desire drove through him, and he swept her up into his arms.

The world tilted on its axis, and her eyes flew open.

Rico's eyes were blazing down at her, vivid even in the low light. Her heart was soaring like a bird in flight, which was strange, because she felt boneless, weak, helpless in his arms as he carried her the few strides to his bed.

He lowered her gently, tenderly, as if she were a delicate, precious flower.

'*Elisabetta*—'

For one long, endless moment he gazed down at her as she lay in a ruffle of silk, one breast exposed, as she looked up at him, wonder and enchantment in her eyes.

Then, with a rapid urgency that was its own message, he'd disposed of his own clothes and was lowering his long, lithe frame upon her. She felt his body crush her down into the softness of the bedding. Felt the strength, the honed, masculine beauty of his planed torso, the narrow circle of his hips, the tautness of his thighs, and the long, full shaft pressing against her.

She gasped, awareness shooting through her.

He saw her recognition.

'I have wanted you,' he breathed, 'from the first moment I saw you. Walking towards me—revealed to me—only to me—in all your beauty.'

Slowly, very slowly, he lowered his head and kissed her. Slowly, very slowly.

'Be mine,' he said to her. 'Be mine, my own Elisabetta .'

His eyes were dilated; she was drowning in their dark depths.

There was only one answer to give him. Only one answer possible.

'Rico…' She breathed his name.

Her arms came around him, closed him to her, her fingers grazing with a fierce, sweet ardour along the contours of his back.

Heat flooded through her. Her hips arched to his. A gesture old as time. The instinctive pleading of her sex. She could not speak, could not talk. She could only know that now, *now* she wanted what was the sweetest glory.

His body answered her. Sliding the silken folds of her dress from her, his hand returned, gliding along the smooth column of her leg, and then, with a touch that drew from her a breathless gasp of pleasure, he parted her.

She was lost—lost in a vortex that was taking her into another world, a world that she had never known existed, to a pleasure, a physical sensation so incredible, that her entire being was reduced to one single exquisite point. She gave herself to it, helpless to do anything but let the ravishing sensation of his skilful touch take her to the place that called to her, nearer and yet nearer, so that when the moment came it was a consummation of discovery, of such wondrous ecstasy that she cried out with it. It swept through her, overwhelming her, flooding through her to her very fingertips, wave after wave. His hand was smoothing her hair, his voice murmuring, and then, even as at last the flood began to ebb, even as she felt the pulsing of her core, he was there, seeking entrance, strong and insistent, and yet with absolute control, easing inside her.

She took him in. The pulsing of her body drew him into her,

and she felt his fullness pressing against her aroused, sensitised tissues. She gasped again, eyes flying open to see him looking down at her, his expression one of absolute focus, one of intensity.

The intensity of desire. Absolute desire.

For her.

Now. *Now.*

He moved within her, and as he did the ebbing fire in her started to lick again. Her lips parted in wonder, and he saw that wonder, and with a brief, flickering smile he moved again. And then, once more, the intensity took him over.

'Yes,' she breathed. 'Yes.' And lifted her hips to him, instinctively tilting to let him move more deeply within her, parting her straining flesh around him, moulding herself around him. He moved again, and yet again, and with each stroke she felt the bliss not just of possession, but of renewed desire.

She heard him speak again, a staccato fragment, and then an urgency took him over. Stroke after stroke, his body surging within her, he took her with him, closer and closer still, to that place where she had been.

And then she was there. Like a white heat sensation flashed through her, sweeping through her limbs. She cried out, and heard his voice too, and she was clutching him, her hands working into the smooth, heated planes of his back, her breath crying through her, her throat arching as the fire took her, took him with her.

It went on and on, until, as the final echo began to ebb, she was left with the sweet, honeyed exhaustion of fulfilment in every fibre of her being. She felt the tautness go from him, felt the full heaviness of his body on hers, and emotion flooded through her. Her arms wrapped around him, her cheek pressing against his. She wanted to hold him close, so close.

Wonder filled her, and a sweetness that was beyond comprehension. She held his warm, strong body in her arms, feeling the hectic beat of his heart gradually slow. His head was sunk against her shoulder. She felt his cheek, his soft, silky hair, the warmth of his breath. His breathing slowed, his muscles relaxing, letting go.

Languor stole through her—a peace so deep that it was like a balm, a blessing. At her hips, still conjoined, she felt his heaviness, felt the low throb within her as her body remembered the imprint of his possession, her own ecstasy. Her languor deepened as her own heart rate slowed, and sleep began to steal over her in her warm, sated drowsiness.

Her hands slackened around his back and she felt his skin begin to cool beneath her fingers. He had slipped over into sleep, she realised, and with the last of her conscious mind she pulled the dishevelled coverlet over him. Then, with a low, soft sigh, she let sleep take her.

'Principessa—je suis enchanté.'

Her hand was being taken, and kissed with courtly gallantry. Lizzy smiled uncertainly. Jean-Paul straightened and bestowed a highly appreciative look at her. He said something in French to Rico, which Lizzy did not understand.

Rico grinned.

'I am indeed,' he replied. 'Incredibly fortunate. And now, if you've finished making up to my bride, let's get on with it. Better start with Ben—before he gets bored with the proceedings.'

But Ben was on his best behaviour, and clearly determined to look angelic, which he did effortlessly, in his smart new clothes.

As for his mother.

Rico's breath caught for the hundredth time.

She sat there, on a sofa in the formal salon of the villa—a room as ornate as the dining room, but ideal for the purpose now—and looked simply—

Radiant.

It was the only word for her, and Rico could not tear his eyes from her.

As Jean-Paul took shot after shot, wonder suffused Rico.

And when it was his turn to be included—first on his own with her, then with Ben, and then with all three of them—although his pose was formal, the look in his eyes was quite different.

At the end of the session, Jean-Paul set his camera aside.

'Bon chance, mon vieux,' he said. 'And I wish you every happiness.'

He clasped Rico's hand, then let it go.

There remained only the business of downloading the digital file from the camera, and offering Jean-Paul the hospitality a friend deserved before he took his leave. And then, while Lizzy took Ben off to change them both into less formal clothes, Rico was left to e-mail Luca.

There was no text. Just a carefully selected attachment.

That would be sufficient.

For a moment after he had hit *send* he just stared at the blank screen.

Then he logged out, and went to find his wife.

She was living in the middle of a dream. A dream so wonderful she knew it could only be a dream. An enchantment. A time out of time.

The whole world seemed suffused with a glow of bliss. Every moment, every instant of every day—and, oh, every night—was filled with a happiness she had never believed possible.

How can I be so happy?

But she did not need to ask. She knew.

Rico—

She had only to breathe his name, only to look at him, hear his voice, take his hand, feel his touch upon her, to know why happiness—deep, profound, immeasurable and infinite—was in every pulse of her blood, every beat of her heart.

She did not want to think, to ask, to question. She wanted only to *be*—to be this wonderful, enchanted person, caught in her blissful, beautiful dream.

It was so strange, she mused. Outwardly, the days passed in

just the same way—easy, undemanding days, a perpetual holiday. Taking Ben down to the beach, swimming in the pool, lounging in the sun, doing everything and nothing, talking about everything and nothing.

And yet everything had changed—changed so utterly she could not believe it, could only float in her haze of wonder and bliss.

By day, the signs were subtle and unconscious—a passing caress, a physical closeness, the casual body language that was the daytime manifestation of intimacy. The hug for Ben that included a hug for her, the little touches of hands as they played with him, the warm, acknowledging glances as they talked and ate and did all the things they had already been doing since they had come to the villa.

But by night—ah, by night her heart lifted in still-incredulous wonder. By night the enchantment that suffused her with a subtle golden haze by day blazed into glory. Glory that burned like stars in its brilliance—glory that melted her body, caress by sweetest caress, touch by sensual touch, stroke by exquisite stroke, until her whole being caught flame and burned like a torch in the ecstasy of her consummation.

His consummation. Because she knew, with every cell of her being, that the strong, virile body she held in her arms, held deep within her own body, was burning too, in the same consummation. She felt his body burn with the same flame, setting him on fire as her arms wrapped him close, and closer still, their bodies fusing as one, until at last the incandescence burned away, leaving them twined about each other in sweet exhaustion.

'How…how can it be so wonderful?' she breathed at him one night, her eyes wide and bemused.

He did not answer, only smoothed her hair, lacing it with his fingers, and cradled her body against his as his hand smoothed along her back, drifting with slow, exhausted sensuousness until it slowed, and slackened, cupping the ripeness of her hip.

He murmured in Italian—words she did not understand but which flowed like honey through her. Like a balm, a blessing.

Then night folded over them and they slept, entwined, embracing. And she dreamt of heaven, because that was where she was already.

Lizzy was creaming his back. Rico lay face down on a lounger. Ben, having surfaced from his siesta, his energy levels renewed, was vigorously batting his way along the length of the pool astride a huge inflatable dolphin.

'Race me,' he called to Rico. 'You can ride the crocodile.' He pointed to a huge, inflatable crocodile with grinning jaws that was floating disconsolately in the shallows.

'Soon,' said Rico, not lifting his head. 'Very soon.'

But not that soon. It was far too good just lying here, with the sun beating down on him, the lightest of breezes playing over his skin, the drowsy sound of the cicadas, the silence of the world around him and Ben splashing happily in the pool, while warm hands glided caressingly, sensuously across his bared back, massaging sun cream deep into the muscled contours, sculpting the bones of his spine, his ribs and shoulders, with smooth, strong strokes.

Well-being, contentment—peace—filled him. He could lie here for ever.

He could be here for ever.

Life was good—so very good.

Everything—everything he wanted was here. Now. An endless now.

Time had stopped. Only day and night existed. Nothing more. There was no world beyond this.

He'd heard nothing yet from his father and Luca—and he didn't care. They belonged in a world he was not interested in right now.

Right now, all he wanted he had. He wanted nothing more.

Footsteps sounded on the shallow flight that led to the upper terrace. A shadow fell over his body. The hands at his back stopped.

He lifted his head and looked up.

Captain Falieri stood there.

Slowly, Rico levered himself up, and stood. Behind him, he could hear Lizzy doing the same. Automatically he felt for her hand and closed his fingers around hers.

'Captain Fally-eery!' Ben's piping voice called with enthusiasm. He splashed his way busily to the steps and clambered out, running up to them. 'Have you come to tea?' he asked convivially.

The Captain shook his head. 'I'm afraid not. I've come—' his eyes flicked to Rico's '—to see your uncle.'

As Falieri looked back at him, Rico could see his gaze moving past him automatically. Even so good a diplomat as he was, he could not, Rico could see, hide the flash of shock in his eyes. He knew why. The woman whose hand he was holding was all but unrecognisable. He felt her slip her hand from his and saw that she was reaching for a sarong to wind about her. Then she was holding out her hand to Ben.

'Let's go and get changed,' she said. 'Captain Falieri,' she acknowledged.

He bowed his head in return, but did not speak. He looked disbelievingly after her as she set off, hand in hand with a protesting Ben.

But Rico was not concerned that his father's chief of police was stunned by the transformation in the appearance of the woman he'd last seen looking so very different in England. He stretched out a hand and picked up his shirt, shrugging it over his shoulders.

'Well?' he asked.

Falieri's eyes snapped back to him.

'His Highness, your father, wishes to see you.'

Rico's mouth pressed together. Then, with a nod of acquiescence, he headed off after Lizzy and Ben.

'Ten minutes,' he called back to Falieri.

It was hard, punishingly hard, to take leave of Lizzy and Ben. But it had to be done. For these past days he had shut out the outside world, ignoring its existence, but that did not stop it existing. Now, he just wanted it sorted.

He took Lizzy's hands. She'd showered and changed, like him, but whereas he had put on a formal suit, knowing his father's preferences, she was wearing a simple sundress. Ben had been peeled out of his trunks and put into shorts and a T-shirt.

'What's going to happen?' He could hear the fear in her voice.

'My father has a very clear choice—he can accept our marriage with outward good grace, and keep everyone happy. Or he can have an open breach with me. I don't care which. Whichever he's chosen, it makes no difference—we're married, you're my wife, Ben is our joint legal charge, and my father *cannot* get his hands on him.' He took a breath. 'I don't want to leave you, but it's the best thing in the circumstances. I don't want you and Ben setting foot in San Lucenzo till all this is settled. I've asked Falieri to stay with you, and he's consented. I trust him. He's not my father's stoolie and he will do *nothing* illegal. He was not involved with the deception my father and brother practised on us at the palace.' His expression darkened. 'It was clever of Luca to send him to England with me—he knows I trust him, and he also knows that Falieri would have refused to be party to their despicable scheme had he been back at the palace.'

'When will you be back?' She was trying to keep her voice steady, he could tell.

'Tonight. There's a helicopter waiting for me at the marina, and the flight won't take long. Nor will whatever my father has to say to me. I'll be heading right back here.'

He gave a sudden smile, dispelling the grimness of his expression.

'Put the champagne on ice, get Ben to bed early, and…' his long lashes swept down over his eyes '…slip into something comfortable.'

For one last moment he held her gaze. Then, letting go her hands, he ruffled Ben's hair and walked out.

Lizzy watched him go. Her chest felt tight.

Ben tugged at her skirt. 'Where's Tio Rico going?' he asked.

'He'll be back later,' said Lizzy absently. She took a breath, trying to focus. 'Let's go and see if Captain Falieri would like a cup of coffee. I'm sure he would.'

'Can he stay to tea, then?' Ben asked, pleased.

'I think he can now. Yes.'

She took Ben out along the terrace. On the far side of the villa she could hear a car moving off, taking Rico down to the heliport.

Captain Falieri walked out of the house. For a moment he seemed a familiar, reassuring figure. Then he turned to look at them as they approached.

There was something in his face that made the blood freeze in her veins.

She stopped in front of him.

'What is it?' Her voice was high, and faint. The tightness in her chest was squeezing hard, so hard.

For a moment he just looked at her. His face was sombre. And in his eyes, most frightening of all, was pity.

'I have,' he said gravely, 'unwelcome news.'

CHAPTER ELEVEN

THE helicopter churned through the air, descending to the palace. Rico must have made this landing a thousand times or more—it was one of the most convenient ways of arriving and departing. He gazed down at the white towers astride the rocky promontory on which the original castle had been built. It was one of the most familiar sights in the world to him.

And yet now it seemed very alien.

He didn't want to do this. He didn't want this confrontation. But it had to be done. And the sooner it was over and done with the better.

Which way had his father chosen? Either Falieri did not know, or he was under strict instructions to give no clue. Well, the waiting would be over very soon, and then Rico would know either the best or the worst.

But it wouldn't be the worst. His father would not risk the scandal of an open breach with his son—he would accept what Rico had done. He wouldn't like it, but he would accept it. For the sake of convention, propriety. For the sake of appearances.

He felt a hardening in his guts. Appearances were all they would be. There could be no real reconciliation with his father. Not after what he had tried to do.

No one, *no one* took a child from its mother. Parted a mother from her child.

No one.

The landing pad soared up to meet them, and there was the familiar jar of impact. The noise of the rotors lessened. Rico released his seat belt, nodded his thanks to the pilot, and slid back the door. Lithely he jumped down and ducked out from under the slowing rotors, then straightened.

As he did, he saw a quartet of figures emerging from the palace. Palace guards in their duty uniforms. He paused, frowning, waiting for them to approach.

'What is it?' he demanded sharply.

The senior officer among them stared straight ahead, not looking at him. His face was expressionless.

'I regret to inform Your Highness,' he said, 'that you are under arrest.'

He was taken to his own apartments. His phone was removed from him, and he realised that all other communication devices, from PC to laptop, had been removed or disabled, including both the house phone and the phones with outside lines.

Disbelief sent shock waves through him.

What the *hell* was going on? Fury, disbelief, shock—all warred within him.

He paced, rigid with rage, across his sitting room.

The double doors opened and he snapped round. The doors had been opened by two of the guards standing outside. Through them was walking his father.

'What the *hell* is this?' Rico demanded.

His father walked in, The guards closed the doors again.

'I have placed you,' said Prince Eduardo, 'under arrest.'

'On what charge?'

Rico's voice was hollow, disbelieving.

There was a silence for a moment. His father's eyes rested on him. They were cold. Rico had never seen them look so cold.

'You have committed a crime against the principality of San Lucenzo.'

His voice was as cold as his eyes.

Rico stared.

'What?'

'It is a crime dating back to medieval times. It has little modern enforcement, with one salient exception.' His father paused again. 'Royal marriages,' he said.

'I don't understand,' Rico answered slowly. He was holding still, very still.

His father's cold eyes rested on him.

'Any member of the royal family requires the consent of the Prince before they may marry. You failed to obtain it. Therefore your marriage is void.'

Rico let the words sink in. Then he spoke.

'You can recognise it after the fact.'

'I shall not do so. The marriage is void. You have married without my consent.'

Rico looked at him.

'Why are you doing this? Does it mean nothing to you that the boy is Paolo's son?' His voice was strange, remote.

'Paolo is dead—because of this boy. Had that greedy, over-ambitious girl not sought to entrap him he would never have lost his life.'

Rico shook his head in denial.

'We know nothing of the nature of their relationship The girl might just as easily have been in love with him, and he with her.'

Something flashed in his father's eyes, and then it was gone. Before he could speak Rico continued.

'And whether or not it was love—or entrapment—Paolo did the honourable thing. He married her for the sake of his unborn child.'

His father's face was like marble. Cold and hard.

'He had no business doing so. His first duty was to his name. He was impetuous and self-indulgent.' His voice grew more heavy. 'I blame myself for that. He was indulged as a child—spoilt—and that was the consequence.'

A chill went down Rico's spine, like ice crystallising in his nerve fibres. His father was speaking again. Rico forced himself to listen.

'Nevertheless, when the existence of the boy was discovered—although I would have preferred to have ignored the matter, whatever repellent drivel the gutter press produced—I was prepared, however reluctantly, to acknowledge Paolo's brief marriage, and thereby accept his son as legitimate. Given the circumstances, it seemed the most…advisable…course of action. With the mother dead there would be no…unwelcome entanglements. The boy would be raised in an appropriate manner, without the indulgence that ruined his father, and accepted as a member of the royal family. Unfortunately the obduracy and ambition of the aunt proved a serious impediment.'

Rico's eyes hardened.

'She is more than his aunt, she is his mother—his legal guardian. I made it crystal-clear that she would not be parted from her son—and your attempt to do so was despicable.'

His father's eyes flashed coldly again.

'You will not address me in such a fashion,' he said freezingly. 'However, you will be glad to learn that the boy is no longer a requirement. I have rescinded my decision to recognise Paolo's marriage.' The cold eyes rested impassively on Rico. 'The boy is therefore illegitimate within the state of San Lucenzo. His future is of no concern to me.'

It was said with an indifference that chilled him to the core.

'He's your grandson,' said Rico. 'Does that mean *nothing* to you?'

His father's face did not change. 'Royal bastards are not acknowledged. He has no entitlements and can have no claim on Paolo's estate. Nevertheless, arrangements will be made for suitable maintenance, and an appropriate capital sum will be settled on him for his majority. The issue is now closed, and I will discuss it no further. Luca will handle the matter with the lawyers, and you will not be involved. As for yourself,' the cold voice continued, 'you will undertake to have no further contact or communication with the woman or the boy. When you have given this undertaking, the charge will be lifted.' He gave a sharp intake of breath. 'That is all I have to say to you.'

Rico looked at him. Looked at this man who was his father.

He was standing only a few metres away from him—but the distance between them was much more than that.

Then, without another word, Prince Eduardo walked from the room.

The doors shut behind him, and Rico was alone once more.

How long he stood there he did not know. He could feel his lungs breathing in, and out, he could feel the steady beat of his heart—but he could not feel anything else.

There were voices outside the doors. A sharp voice, and then a deferential one. A door swung open—only one this time.

It was Luca.

Rico looked at him. For a long moment the brothers' eyes met and held.

'Why did you do it?' There was almost resignation in his brother's voice as he put the question, Rico thought. 'Are you completely insane—or just extraordinarily stupid? Not just to do what you have, but then to think you could pressurise our father into accepting it. Good God, do you not know him well enough by now to know he would *never* back down before you?'

'I thought he would consider the scandal of an open breach with me more repugnant than forcing himself to do the decent thing by Paolo's son.'

'The decent thing?' A dam seemed to break inside Luca. 'God Almighty, Rico. You've lost us Paolo's son. His *son*. Do you know, do you have *any idea*, how hard I had to work to get our father to recognise Paolo's marriage? When I told him that there was a story brewing in the press, and what it was, his first and immediate reaction was to ignore it. He was so furious with Paolo that he couldn't think straight. But he finally agreed— after endless persuasion on my part—that the best thing to do would be to recognise the boy as legitimate. That meant he

could come here. That meant he *had* to come here. On his own,' he spelt out. 'That went without saying. Do you seriously imagine for a moment that our father would have anything to do with the family of the boy's mother?'

Luca's mouth set grimly. 'But how the hell could I have known that the girl would kick up such a fuss, and that you— *you* of all people—would let her get away with it? *Dio*, Rico— *you* were the one who was supposed to have her eating out of your hand, not the other damn way round. I never had you down for an idiot—let alone an insane one—but I do now. And now, thanks to your insane stupidity, you've gone and lost us Paolo's son. Thanks to you he's been declared a bastard. A bastard— Paolo's son. *That's* what you've achieved. And it's not something I'm going to forgive you for lightly.'

Bitter fury stung in his accusation. Then his slate eyes flashed again.

'It's time to grow up, Rico. To take some responsibility. Not to play infantile games and be led around by your damn over-active sex-drive! Because that's what's happened, obviously. That much is clear from the photos you sent. You had her done up and moved in on her. Well, I hope you've had your fill of her—because it's over now. You won't be allowed to go within a hundred miles of her. From now on she doesn't exist any more. And maybe finally you'll *learn* some responsibility, Rico. You'd better, because this really is your last chance. He's made that very clear, our father—very clear indeed. You came *this* close to stepping over the edge. This close. From now on, no more stepping out of line by you—not one more *breath* of scandal. From now on you learn to conduct yourself with some responsibility.'

He fell silent, his eyes heavy on his brother.

'Responsibility?' said Rico slowly. His eyes rested on Luca. Nothing showed in them. 'I've always had a problem with responsibility. Because I never had any. My sole responsibility was to stay alive, that was all. In case you dropped dead. Turned out gay. Refused to marry. Proved infertile. And in the meantime, until and unless any of that happened, I passed the time. Any way I could. Because that was all I *could* do. All I was allowed to do. Pass the time. However pointlessly. Until—' his voice changed '—until I found out there was something I could do, after all. Something, in fact, that only I could do— no one else could. I could save Paolo's son.'

His eyes never left Luca's, not for an instant, boring into him, burning into him. 'I could save Paolo's son from the hellish childhood that was being cooked up for him. The one you told me about when I delivered Ben and his mother into your tender hands like a fool—the fool you'd played me for. You wanted to throw his mother away like garbage and condemn Ben to a childhood that was going to be even worse than the one we had, Luca. Do you remember our childhood? Do you? Or has that just conveniently been blanked out of your memory? Because it hasn't from mine, and there was no way—no way on this earth—that I was going to let that happen to Paolo's son. There was no way that I was going to let him be taken from the woman he regards as his mother, *loves* as his mother, or let her lose her child. I could stop it happening—and I did. And I don't regret it for one second. Not one instant.' His voice was a low snarl now. 'Even though I've discovered just what kind of callous *scum* you all are.'

He took a harsh intake of breath. 'And now, if you don't want me to knock you out cold again, I suggest you get the hell out of my quarters.'

He saw his brother's lip twist.

'Thinking to use your *Boy's Own* secret passage and head for the hills again, Rico? It won't do you any good this time. It won't get you out of the hole you're in now. You've run out of options. Your marriage has been declared void, and you're under arrest.'

Rico's mouth whitened.

'I don't give a—'

'Allow me,' bit out Luca, cutting through the expletive, 'to explain to you exactly what San Lucenzan law in respect of royal marriages allows the Prince Regnant to do.'

In precise, exact and comprehensive terms, he did so.

Rico listened. And as he listened, his face slowly froze.

Lizzy was sitting very still. Very still indeed. She had sent Ben to the playroom, telling him to watch a DVD until she came for him.

'I am so very sorry,' Captain Falieri was saying, 'to be the bearer of such…unsettling…news, Miss Mitchell.'

Lizzy said nothing. What could she say? Yet she had to say something.

She swallowed. There seemed to be a stone in her throat.

'So…so what happens now? To Ben and me?'

Her voice was thin, and she was trying to stop it shaking.

Captain Falieri was being kind—so very kind. Somehow that just made it worse.

'I am to escort you both back to Cornwall. Perhaps you would instruct the staff to pack what you intend to take? Needless to say, all…' he hesitated minutely '…all personal effects purchased for your stay here will be considered yours.'

She said nothing. She would allow Ben to choose his favourites from amongst the toys that he had acquired here. As for herself…

She felt her heart crushed, as if heavy weights were squeezing it.

She would need nothing. Nothing but what she had arrived with.

She got to her feet. The motion was jerky.

'If you will excuse me—?'

'Of course. However…' The minute hesitation came again. 'Before you go, I am instructed to require you to sign a particular document.'

He drew a thick, long envelope from his inside breast

pocket and took out the folded document within. He placed it in front of her.

'Although you may wish to read it first—there is a translation attached to the original, as you can see—its content is very straightforward. His Highness, Prince Eduardo, requires you to agree to certain…restrictions. You are to make no claim either on your behalf, or that of your nephew, on the estate of his late natural father, or upon His Highness's estate. You are to have no contact with the press in any way. All approaches by any member of the press to you, you are to direct to His Highness's press secretary to deal with. You are to undertake never to agree to or participate in the publication of any book, or the broadcast of any programme, in any medium, pertaining to your nephew. When these undertakings have been agreed by yourself, a regular sum will be paid to you, for the maintenance of yourself and your nephew. When your nephew achieves his majority, a capital sum will be settled on him by His Highness, in due recognition of the financial obligation that would have devolved upon your nephew's natural father.'

He fell silent and extracted a fountain pen from his inside jacket, placing it beside the document, formally opening it to the final page, where her signature was to be appended.

'I will sign the papers,' said Lizzy. 'But I will not accept any money. Please make that very clear to His Highness.'

She put her signature to the document and waited while Captain Falieri added his own, as witness.

Then she turned away. 'I must talk to my son,' she said.

Gravely, Captain Falieri inclined his head, and watched her walk out.

Rain was falling. Heavy, relentless sheets of rain that swept in off the North Atlantic, rattling against the windowpanes, spitting down the chimney.

The cottage felt cold, so cold.

Damp and unused.

Captain Falieri's expression darkened as he brought her cases indoors.

'You cannot stay here,' he said bluntly. 'I will take you to a hotel.'

Lizzy shook her head.

'No. I would rather be here. I'll be all right.'

She turned to him and held out her hand.

'Thank you,' she said. 'For doing what you could to make this as…simple…as possible.'

He took her hand, but he did not shake it. Instead, he bowed over it.

'I wish…' he said, and he straightened and looked into her eyes. 'I wish that matters had been…otherwise.'

Her throat tightened. She could not cope with kindness.

Nor with pity.

'Thank you,' she said again. 'You had better go now. I'm sure the pilot will wish to start his return flight.'

A private plane had flown her to a military airfield further south, and then Captain Falieri had driven her and Ben to her cottage.

'If you are sure?'

She nodded. 'It would be best for Ben.' She swallowed. 'A complete break will be the easiest for him. As it was when—'

She could not continue. Memories pressed upon her, heavy and unbearable. Could it really have only been a few weeks ago that she had stood here in the hallway admitting entrance to two strangers?

She felt the vice close around her heart again.

She turned and went into the kitchen. Ben was sitting at the table, slumped over it, dejection in every line.

'Captain Falieri has to go now, Ben. Come and say goodbye.'

Ben lifted his face to her.

'Can't we go back with him, Mummy? Can't we? I don't like it here. It's cold.' There were tears in his voice. The vice inside her crushed even more tightly.

'No, my darling, we've come home now. Our holiday is over.'

Tears quivered in Ben's eyes.

'I don't want it to be over,' he said.

There was nothing she could say. Nothing at all. She wanted to sit at the table and howl with him, pour out all her grief and heartbreak. But she could not. She had to be strong for Ben.

She forced a smile to her lips.

'All holidays end, Ben. Now, come and say goodbye to Captain Falieri. He's been kind to us. Very kind.' She felt her voice crack dangerously.

She took Ben's hand and led him dejectedly out into the hallway.

'Goodbye, Ben,' said Captain Falieri gravely. He held out a hand to him.

Ben did not take it.

'Am I really not a prince any more, Captain Fally-eery?' His eyes were wide and pleading.

The Captain shook his head. 'I'm afraid not, Ben.'

'And Mummy isn't a princess?'

'No.'

'It was only for the holiday, Ben. Us being a prince and princess,' said Lizzy. It was the only way she had been able to explain it to Ben.

'What about Tio Rico? Isn't he a prince any more?'

Lizzy's hand rested on his shoulder. It tightened involuntarily.

'He will always be a prince, my darling. Nothing can change that.'

For one long, terrible moment she met Captain Falieri's eyes. Then looked away.

She waited as he took his leave, walking out into the rain. She heard the car door open, then slam shut, and the engine rev. The car drove off down the lane to the coast road, heading back to the airfield, to the waiting plane that would take him away.

She shut the door as a spatter of rain came in on the wind.

She shivered.

'Let's light a fire, Ben. That will warm things up.'

But she would never be warm again, she knew. A terrible, deathly chill embraced her.

How am I going to bear this? How?

The question rang out in her anguish, but she had no answer. There could be no answer.

She went into the kitchen. Captain Falieri had very kindly stopped at a supermarket on the way from the airfield and bought some provisions for her. They would do until she could get to the shops. Mechanically she started to unpack them, and then put some milk to heat on the electric cooker. Warm milk would be good for Ben. They had eaten on the plane; it had helped to make the journey pass. It wasn't really very late, though the rain made it seem darker. Only a few hours since they had left the villa. Only a few hours…

She stilled, unable to move. It was like a physical pain convulsing through her.

With all her strength she forced herself to continue, to make up the fire in the range, set it to draw, check the heat of the milk.

Ben sat at the table, head sunk upon his arms, a picture of misery.

I've got to keep going. It's all I can do. Just keep going. Keep going.

It became her mantra. The only thing that got her through the evening, got her through the following day. And the one after that. And it would get her through the one after that. All the days that stretched ahead of her.

For the rest of her life.

It was unbearable—yet she had to bear it.

There's nothing else. Nothing else I can do. Just keep going. It will pass. Eventually it will pass.

It had to.

Eventually it will get better. Eventually I will accept it. Accept what happened.

That for a brief golden time I was there, with him.

And that time was over. Never to return.

She looked around her, at the worn, shabby interior of the cottage. So short a time ago all she had wanted in the world was to be back here, without her life turned upside down, with Ben just an ordinary child, living a normal life with her.

She would have given anything for that.

Be careful what you pray for...

The old adage came back to haunt her.

The nights were the worst. The nights were agony. Hour after hour she stared into the dark. Remembering.

It's all I have. Memories.

Memories that were vivid, agonising. But memories that she knew, with even greater anguish, would start to fade. Like old photos, the colour seeping from them year by year. They would become blurred and lost. Gone for ever.

Just as he was gone for ever from her life.

Her thoughts reached for him, reached through the silence and the dark, reached across the sea and the land.

But where he was she did not know.

And what would it matter if you did? What would it matter if you could see him where he is? His world has taken him back—to the life he had, the life he has again. You were an...intermission...for him. He did what he did to keep Ben safe—and now Ben is safe again. Ben does not need him. He can have his own life back, as Ben has his.

As you have yours.

Without him.

Only memories. Memories to last a lifetime. Nothing more than memories.

A damp sun struggled through the clouds. After days of rain, the overcast skies were clearing. Raindrops dazzled drippingly on the branches of the trees, and a milder wind creamed up the coombe, bringing the scent of the sea.

'Come on, Ben, let's go down to the beach.'

With forced jollity she rallied him, filling her voice with an enthusiasm she did not feel. Nor did she meet with any in return.

'I don't want to,' said Ben. 'I want to go back to Tio Rico's beach.'

'Other people are having their holiday there now,' she said. 'It's like here in Cornwall. People come for a holiday, and then they go home. That's quite sad for them, isn't it? We live here all the time—so that's good.'

Ben looked at her mutinously.

'We could live in the house by Tio Rico's beach all the time,' he said.

'That house was only for a holiday for us. This is the house we live in. And we're very lucky to be here, Ben. Lots of people have to live in cities, where there isn't any beach at all.'

'I don't like the beach here. It hasn't got a swimming pool. And it hasn't got Tio Rico.' Ben's lower lip wobbled.

'The beach here has got waves,' said Lizzy, with determined cheerfulness.

'But it hasn't got Tio Rico,' Ben protested. He swallowed, and lifted his eyes to her. 'Mummy, doesn't Tio Rico want us any more?

She tried to find the words. Words that a four-year-old child could make sense of. But they were cruel words, harsh words for all that. Yet what else could she do except say them? To give Ben false hope would be the cruellest thing of all.

'Your uncle can't be with us any more, Ben,' she began carefully. 'He has duties to attend to. He has to be a prince now, not an uncle. It was just a holiday we spent with him. Just a holiday. That's all.'

Her words fell with excruciating mockery into her own ears.

A holiday. That was all it had been. A holiday of enchantment, magic, wonder, and such bliss that it made the realisation that such a time could never come again so agonising that she could hardly bear it.

But above all, above everything else, she must not say the words that ached to be said. For what was the use of saying them? What was the use, even in the dark—all alone in the bed she had once been content to lie in, solitary, celibate, untouched by the magic that he had strewn over her—what was the use, sleepless and despairing, of letting those words whisper in her mind, each one an agony of loss?

The only way she could face the rest of her life now was never, ever, to say those words. Never even to think them. Or they would destroy her.

Resolutely, she went on getting the beach things together.

Pain and memory clawing within her.

She took Ben, protesting, down to the beach. She had forgotten how chill the wind could be even at this time of year, in early summer. She made a camp in the lee of a line of rocks, sedimentary shales turned on their side by vast geological forces over vast reaches of time. So much time.

She looked out to sea.

Where was he now? she wondered. Was he in some fashionable high-society resort—Monte Carlo, the Caribbean, somewhere exotic? Mingling with fashionable high-society people? Fashionable high-society women, every one a beauty, the kind that he took his pick of—the Playboy Prince, leading the life he was born to lead?

Stop it. It doesn't matter.

It doesn't matter where he is, or who he's with, or what he's doing.

It doesn't matter.

It will never matter again, for the rest of your life.

She shook out the rug and weighted down the corners with a book, shoes and a bag.

'Who's for a paddle?' she said, forcing her voice to be cheerful.

'It's too cold,' said Ben, and sat on the rug and wrapped a towel around him.

She whisked it off.

'Then we'll make a railway track. Which engines did you bring down with you?'

'I don't want trains—I want my fort. The fort Tio Rico made with me.'

Lizzy's heart sank. Gently she said, 'We couldn't bring it back, Ben. It was too big—don't you remember? But we brought the knights, so that's good, isn't it?' she finished encouragingly.

'But it's the *fort* I want. Tio Rico and me made it. We made it together, and it had a bridge and a porcully and towers.'

She felt her heart catch with pain. Like a knife slicing into her memory stabbed her and she was there again, in the warmth and the sunshine—the ugly sister who had so miraculously been turned into Cinderella. Sleeping Beauty ready to be kissed awake by the most handsome Prince in the world.

No. Anguish crushed her. She mustn't let herself think, remember. It was gone, all gone. Like a dream. An enchantment.

A fairytale that was over now.

She took a breath.

She must not think of fairytales. They were just that. Unreal. This was real—here, now. With Ben. She chivvied him along, refusing to let him mope. What was the point of him moping? What was the point of her moping? They had to get on with things. They had to.

They had to keep going.

'Well, we haven't got the fort any more, but we have got trains. So let's start building this track,' she said, with forced resolution.

She started digging into the sand, carving out the railway tracks that Ben liked to make so that he could drive his engines along. The sand was cold beneath the surface, and wet. The sand at the villa had been warm, dry.

And Rico had helped Ben make the tracks.

'Come on, Ben, give me a hand,' she said.

Morosely he started to help, his expression unhappy. Lizzy

ignored it. She had to. She had to jolly him along, get him cheerful again, enthusiastic again. What alternative was there? She knelt down on the sand, facing out to sea, letting the wind whip her hair into unflattering frizzled wisps.

Her looks were going already, she knew. Without all the expensive attentions of stylists and beauticians she was beginning to revert. She didn't care.

What did Ben care what she looked like?

And there was no one else to care.

Never again.

'Where shall we make the train station?' she asked, kneeling back a moment, feeling the wind-blown sand stinging on her cheeks.

'Don't care,' said Ben. He sat back as well, beside her. 'It's a stupid, stupid track, and I don't care where the stupid, stupid station is. Stupid, stupid, *stupid.*' He bashed the sand with his spade, spattering it in all directions.

'Well, I'd put it just before the branch line goes off, Ben. That's the place for a station.'

The voice that spoke was deep and accented, and it came from behind them.

CHAPTER TWELVE

THE world seemed to stop. Stop completely. Except that it didn't stop. It whirled around her. Whirled with a dizzying speed that made her feel faint.

It wasn't possible. It was an illusion—an auditory illusion. They happened sometimes—you could hear people speaking who weren't there.

Who were somewhere quite different. Who were at some aristocratic house party somewhere, or on a multimillion-pound yacht, or flying in a private jet to a tropical island with a beautiful film star for company.

Who weren't on a Cornish beach, with the wind blowing off the North Atlantic. Making the wind feel as if it was being wafted there from paradise...

Her vision dimmed. She felt clouds rushing in from all around. The blood was thick in her head, bowing her down with its weight.

'Tio Rico!'

Ben's voice was alight. She could hear it, piercing through the clouds and the thickening blood.

'Tio Rico. Tio Rico!'

She bowed her head. It was impossible. Impossible.

'Hello, Ben? Have you been good without me?'

'No,' shouted Ben. Excitement overwhelmed him. 'You weren't here. Why weren't you here, Tio Rico?'

'I got delayed. I'm sorry. But I'm here now.' She felt him lower himself down on to the rug. And still she could not move. Not a muscle.

'Are you going to stay?' Ben demanded. But there was fear in his voice.

'As long as you want me to stay.' He paused. 'If your mother agrees, that is. Do you?'

His hand was on her shoulder. Warm and strong. Sending heat through her, a living warmth that she could not bear.

'Lizzy?'

She looked up. He was only a foot or two away from her, hunkered down on the rug. She saw him immediately, completely. She saw everything about him in one absolute moment. As if he had always been there.

'You shouldn't be here,' she said. Her voice was thick, as thick as the blood suffocating her veins. 'Captain Falieri explained to me. He said you would not be allowed to see Ben again.'

The expression in his eyes altered.

'Well, that depends,' he said. He was looking at her very deeply, very strangely, right into her eyes.

'No, it doesn't,' she said. 'It doesn't depend at all. He said it very clearly. He explained it very clearly. You're not allowed to see Ben any more.'

From the corner of her eye she could see Ben's face pucker.

'Why can't Tio Rico see me any more?' he said.

She saw Rico reach out and ruffle Ben's hair.

'Your mother's got it wrong. I'm here, aren't I?'

It was her turn for her face to pucker.

'But you *shouldn't* be,' she said fiercely. 'You *can't* be.'

His expression changed again. Something entered his eyes. Something she didn't want to see.

'Where else should I be,' he asked quietly, but with deadliness in his voice, 'but with my wife and my boy?'

'No,' she said. She rocked forward slightly. Denying it. Denying it completely. 'No,' she said again.

He looked at her. Looked at her with eyes that chilled her to the bone.

'Did you really think,' he asked, in that same quiet, deadly tone, 'that I would stay away?'

She snapped upright.

'You've got to go!' she shouted at him. 'You've got to go—right away. Right now. Falieri told me. He *told* me. So go—*go.*'

There was a steely glint in his eye. He reached for her hands and hauled her down again. Her eyes were wild, desperate.

'He told me,' she said, and there was despair in her voice. 'He told me everything. He told me about that law—the one that says you can't marry without the Ruling Prince's permission. He told me that it meant our marriage was null and void.'

'Our marriage is real, Lizzy. We made our vows in front of a priest. No one can overturn that.' Steel was in his voice now.

'Yes, they can. They can. Your father can overturn it—and that's what he's done.'

'All my father can do is refuse to recognise our marriage within San Lucenzo. He cannot overturn it. He has no power over our marriage, Lizzy. None.' He spoke steadily, remorselessly.

Her face contorted. 'Yes, he has. He *has.* Captain Falieri told me—he told me quite clearly. He's got absolute power over you. You've broken the law, and if you don't obey him he'll use that power. And he'll do it. Captain Falieri said he would do it.' She swallowed. The stone in her throat was agony. But she spoke, saying the words that had been burnt into her like an agonising brand.

'He'll do it, Rico—he'll strip you of your royalty. He'll disinherit you. He'll disbar you from the succession. Take you off the Civil List, freeze all your assets in San Lucenzo. He'll take everything from you—everything. He'll leave you with nothing.'

She heard Captain Falieri's voice tolling in her head. Saying the words that had taken everything from *her.* All hope. Gone for ever. They had crushed her, crushed her heart, cracking it in pieces.

There was a strange look on Rico's face. It frightened her. His expression was calm. Very calm. Far too calm.

'Falieri was wrong. There was something my father could not take from me.' He paused. Then he spoke. 'You. He could not take you from me. My wife.'

Her face contorted again.

'No. *No.*'

'You are my wife, and Ben is my adopted son, and no one— no power on earth—will take you from me.'

She twisted her hands in his grip.

'No,' she cried again. Her eyes were anguished. 'You mustn't say that. I won't let you. I won't. You've got to go now. Right now.'

He gave a sudden laugh, gripping her hands more tightly yet.

'What a venal woman you are,' he said. 'You only want me for my title, don't you?' His fingers slid into hers. 'Well, I've bad news for you, Signora Ceraldi—'

'Don't say that. Just go. It's not too late.'

He hauled her against him, crushing her against the hard wall of his chest.

'It's far too late. Far, far too late.'

He kissed her.

The kiss went on and on. And she drowned in it. Drowned in his arms. Drowned in the tears pouring from her.

'Mummy—Mummy?'

A little hand was tugging at her arm. Ben's voice was confused, bewildered. Rico half let her go. He swept Ben to him.

'Now, tell me—tell me true.' He stood him up in the crook of his arm, hugging his little body close to him. His other arm was wrapped tight around Lizzy. 'Which would you rather? Me not at all—or me not as a prince but still you and me and Mummy?'

'Would you go away again?' Ben asked.

Rico shook his head. 'Never. Unless you came with me. I might go sometimes—just to work, that sort of thing—maybe for the day or a few days. But you would live with me, and so would Mummy. Would that be any good?'

'Where would we all live?'

'Anywhere you liked. Well, except in a palace.'

'I want to live here and at the holiday house with the swimming pool,' Ben stipulated. 'With you and Mummy. For ever and ever.'

'Done,' said Rico. 'High five says yes.'

Ben gave him a high five. 'Yes,' he shouted. 'Yes, yes, *yes*.'

His little face was alight—alight with joy.

Lizzy's face was wet with tears.

'You can't do this. You just *can't*,' she sobbed.

Rico's arm tightened around her shaking shoulders.

'Too late,' he told her. 'Done deal.' He kissed her forehead softly. 'Done deal, Signora Ceraldi.' His eyes gazed into hers. Deep, deep eyes. 'Now, don't go and tell me it was just the royal bit you fell for?' His voice was admonishing. 'My ego won't take it, you know. It really won't.'

She swallowed, hard. 'Ben—' her voice was shaky '—why not start on that station now? Tio Rico and I need to talk. Boring grown-up stuff.'

'OK,' said Ben.

His world was restored. Happily, he scrambled back onto the sand and started scooping it up to shape into a railway station. Carefully, very carefully, Lizzy undraped herself and pulled away, to the far edge of the rug.

'You can't do this,' she said again. She made her voice steady. Very steady. Calm and rational. 'I won't let you. I won't let you give everything up for Ben. He's young. He'll soon forget you. It will be hard at first, but in a year he'll have for-gotten you. You'll just be a memory, and even that will fade.'

He was looking at her strangely. Then he spoke.

'But, you see, my memories of Ben won't fade. *I* won't forget *him*. And I won't give him up. He's my brother's son—and as clearly as if Paolo were here now I can hear him telling me to be the father to Ben that he was not allowed to be. Just as you—' he made each word telling '—are the mother to Ben that your sister was not allowed to be. And though the cruelty of their deaths can never be assuaged, we know that we can be the loving family to their son that he needs. Because we both love him—and we love each other, don't we, Lizzy?'

She opened her mouth, but no words came. He supplied them for her.

'You can't kiss a man like you just did unless you love him. You can't cry all over a man like you just did unless you love him. And you certainly can't tell a prince he's not to give up his title for the woman he loves unless you love him. I've got you on all three counts, Signora Ceraldi. And I've got you on more counts than that. An infinite number—not just every night we were together, but every moment we were together. Every look, every touch, everything we said to each other, every meal we shared—every smile we shared, everything.'

He shook his head ruminatively. 'It started right from the beginning—even though I didn't know it. Seeing you with Ben, seeing you love him and care for him. And when…' He paused, then went on, 'When you used that horrible, cruel word about yourself, describing our marriage, I wanted to do anything, *everything* I could to banish it.' His eyes softened. 'And I had my reward—oh, I did indeed. Ever since you walked towards me along that terrace, looking such a knockout, taking my breath away, I've been lost. And I know that makes me sound superficial and trivial, thinking with my Y chromosome, but you bowled me over. Blew me away. Knocked me for six. Whatever you want to call it—I went for it.' His voice changed again. 'But it isn't just because of that. It can't be—because even now, when you haven't got a scrap of make-up on, and your hair is going frizzy again, and God alone knows what rubbish dump you got that T-shirt out of, I just want to hold you and never, *never* let you go again. Why do you suppose that is?'

She fingered a corner of the rug and wouldn't look at him.

'It was just novelty. Kindness. Something like that.'

Rico said a word in Italian. She didn't know what it meant, but she could tell it wasn't one she wanted Ben to copy.

'It was love. Do you know how I know? Because when I heard my father telling me my marriage was void I wanted to hit him. Pulverise him.'

'He was trying to manipulate you. No wonder you were angry.'

'He was trying to take me away from you. And I wasn't going to let him.'

'He was trying to take you away from Ben.'

'Ben, yes—and *you*. Stop trying to tell me I don't love you, Signora Ceraldi.' He shook his head again, and only the glint in his eyes told her his jibe was not cruel. 'What a low opinion you have of me. The Playboy Prince—that's all you think of me, isn't it? Admit it.'

She could find no humour in it. 'You can't give up your birthright.' Her voice was low, and vehement. 'You can't.'

'I can and I have. Like I said, it's a done deal. It was a done deal the moment my self-righteous brother informed me what the penalty for my crime was. It took a while,' he said grimly, 'to convince Luca and my father that I was serious in the answer I gave them. That there was no way on God's earth that I would repudiate you and agree to void our marriage—and to hell with their damn laws. But finally they washed their hands of me. I've signed God knows how many documents my father had drawn up, and now, finally, I've been able to come to you.'

She shook her head urgently, violently.

'No. I won't let you. I won't let you do this, Rico. *Please* go back. Go back before it's too late. You can get your title restored, be reinstated, go back on the Civil List, unfreeze your San Lucenzan assets—'

But he only laughed, lounging back on the rug, propped up on one elbow. 'Yes, definitely a venal woman, Signora Ceraldi.' He gave an extravagant sigh. 'I'm only good enough for you when I'm a royal, and I'm only good enough for you when I've got my fingers in the San Lucenzan royal coffers.'

He shook his head sorrowfully. 'My sweet little gold-digger—don't you realise that since I turned eighteen it has been my life-long ambition never to be strung up by the family financial umbilical cord? I know you think I'm just a mindless Playboy Prince, but I haven't spent my youth simply philandering and racing powerboats and the like. I've made investments, taken financial interests in various ventures, played the stock markets. I may not be worth quite what I was before I quit San Lucenzo, but we can jog along quite comfortably, I promise you. We may even—' his eyes glinted again, making weakness wash through her '—run to buying that villa in Capo d'Angeli. Would you like that? But let's keep your cottage here. We'll do it up properly. Put central heating in. I'd like to spend time here. The surf looks good.'

Her hands twisted in her lap.

'The water's far too cold for you here.'

He took her hands and untwisted them. 'Then I look forward to you warming me up afterwards. Will you do that, hmm?' The glint turned into a gleam. The weakness washed through her again.

Then he was smoothing the fingers of her hands—softly, sensuously.

'Too many days without you,' he was murmuring. 'Too many nights. What a lot we have to make up for.'

She took a deep breath. Looked him right in the eyes. Those dark, beautiful, long-lashed eyes.

'Rico, don't do this. Please don't do this. I can't bear it.'

The long sooty lashes swept down over his eyes, then back up again.

'And I can't bear not to. It's as simple as that.'

For one long, endless moment he just looked into her eyes, her face, searching for her—finding her.

A little hand was tugging at him. With a lithe, fluid movement Rico jackknifed up to a sitting position.

'What's up, Ben?' he said smilingly.

'Tio Rico,' asked Ben speculatively, 'did you remember to bring the fort we made?'

It took Ben a long time to settle for bed that night. He bounced around in a state of over-excitement, until finally he could fight sleep no more. Carefully, Rico made his way down the narrow, creaking stairs, ducking his head under the low lintel. The door to the kitchen was open, and she was sitting there, a mug of tea in her cupped hands, staring sightlessly.

How long would it take her to believe? he wondered. Believe that he knew exactly what he was doing, regretted nothing. And would never regret.

He walked in, and her eyes flew to him instantly, unswervingly. And he saw in them such a blaze that it took his breath away.

Where had it come from, this love he felt for her? He didn't know. It had just arrived, that was all. Some time when he wasn't paying attention. When he was just being with her. With Ben.

My family, he thought. That's who they are. My wife and my boy. My son. I'll be the father he couldn't have. I'll take care of him. So simple. So easy. It had been no choice at all.

'Asleep,' he announced. 'Finally.'

'He's excited,' she said. While he'd been settling Ben she'd tried to do something with her appearance, he could tell. She'd put some make-up on, styled her hair. She looked good. Not as glossy, not as stunning as she had when she'd gone for the full works, but good. Definitely good.

The strange thing was, he didn't care.

I love her stunning, I love her plain.

Because I just love—her.

He sat himself down on the table, just by her.

'There's still time to change your mind. You could still go back.'

He smiled. It was a strange smile. Filled with humour, with resignation, with understanding.

'I'm here for good, Lizzy. You've just got to accept it.'

'I can't. That's what I can't do. Rico, it was just a dream—an enchantment. I was Cinderella at the ball, dancing with the Prince. Sleeping Beauty being woken by the Prince's kiss. Fairytales. That's all.'

He looked down at her. 'Has it never occurred to you that the Prince in the fairytale might like a fairytale of his own? One where he gets to quit being a prince all the time? Do you know—' his voice changed, his expression changed '—that you are the only person in my entire life to look at me and see me? Not a prince. Me.'

A look of confusion passed over her face. He gave a rueful smile. 'You don't remember, do you? But I do. I stood in this very cottage and told you we had to run from the paparazzi. And you kept saying why? Why did we have to run? Because you hadn't the faintest idea who I was. Not a clue. You just saw some man bossing you about for no good reason. Not a prince. Not the Playboy Prince. Not the spare Prince to understudy the Crown Prince. Just some man who was trying to boss you about. And even when you knew I was a prince you never really knew how to behave with me, did you? You never called me Highness, or Sir, or anything. The whole royalty thing just…passed you by.'

She still looked troubled, her hands tightening around her mug. 'It doesn't matter what I thought. Rico, you've been royal all your life—'

'And much good it's done me,' he interrupted her. 'Listen, Lizzy—I'm a lot like you.' His eyes were serious, holding hers intently. 'Like you, all my life I've been—unnecessary. Just as you were. To your parents, only your sister was important. To mine, only the heir was important. The spare was just that—spare. Only with Paolo did they ever seem to realise they had a son—not a ruling prince-in-waiting. They lavished on Paolo the love they weren't able to lavish on Luca and me. I don't know what screwed your parents up—because they *were* screwed up, Lizzy, badly, and they'd done an ace job of screwing you up too, until I got you out of that box they'd nailed you into—but I know what screwed mine up: being royal. I did a lot of thinking when I was put under house arrest by my own father, and it always came back to that. Maybe it's different for Luca—he has, after all, something to do, something to look forward to doing. But me—well, I never had anything useful to do. I represented my father or Luca from time to time, attended a few Great Council meetings, signed a few state papers when my father was ill and Luca abroad. But I was never really needed.'

He touched the side of her cheek with a finger.

'You and Ben are the first people that ever needed me,' he said. 'Just like Ben was the first person ever to need *you*, Lizzy. He gave your life meaning and purpose. And that's what you and he do for me. Give my life meaning and purpose. That's why,' he said very softly, his eyes darkening, 'we belong together.'

She was silent. She couldn't say anything. But her eyes slipped away from him. In her chest a hard, heavy lump was forming.

'What is it?' he asked, in that same quiet voice.

The lump hardened, and speaking over it was painful, impossible. But she made herself do it.

'You're offering me a life I can't accept.'

He frowned. 'Why can't you accept it?' he asked, his voice still low.

She swallowed. The lump did not go away.

'Because I shouldn't have it,' she said. 'Because it should be Maria's life. She was the one a prince fell in love with. She was the one who should have been a princess. She was the one Ben should have belonged to. Not me. *Not me.* I took Ben from her. I told the doctors to turn off her life support after Ben had been delivered, after he had grown to term inside a mother whose brain had died weeks earlier. I told them to kill my sister so I could have her baby for myself.'

Huge, anguished eyes looked at him. Her fingers were pressed so tight around the mug they showed white all the way through.

'I told them to do it.'

Carefully he got to his feet. Carefully he hunkered down beside her, placing a hand, warm and strong, on her thigh.

'There was no one else to tell them,' he said. 'Your parents had made their decision. They had gone, taken their way out, leaving *you* with that decision. Making *you* the scapegoat for that decision. They didn't even have the courage, the *love* to stay alive for their grandson's sake. Let alone for yours. And tell me something, Lizzy—tell me from your heart. Do you think your sister would have wanted to live on, in body only, while Paolo was already dead? Their deaths were a tragedy—each and every death that night a tragedy. But *we* are *not* responsible. All we can do is go on with our own lives—and remember theirs. So let's take Ben, you and me, and bring him up in a happy family. We can't change the past—but we can make the future. Together, Lizzy. *Together.*'

He reached and wrapped his arms around her, very close. Slowly she let go of the mug. Slowly she slid her arms around him, burying her face in his shoulder.

'Be happy, Lizzy. Let yourself be happy. With me. For now, and for all our lives together. Life isn't certain—we both know that. So more than anything we must live while we can—for Ben and for each other. And perhaps...' His hand slid across her stomach, warm and seeking. 'Perhaps for one or two more. Ben needs a family—brothers and sisters. Happy and loving, all together.'

He drew her to her feet. Kissed her softly. Then not so softly.

As he drew back she saw the glint deep in his dark, lambent eyes. She felt her heart turn over. The glint turned to a gleam. The gleam to a look that melted her bones.

'Come, Signora Ceraldi, time for bed. I want to find out whether it was just my title you fell for.'

Her arms went around him. Holding him tight, so very tight. Close against her.

'Prince of my heart,' she whispered. 'Love of my life. My adored, beloved husband.'

'Sounds good,' he said. 'Sounds very good.'
He kissed her once more, and then again.
And then he led her upstairs, to the bliss that awaited them.

EPILOGUE

THE photos that Jean-Paul had taken at the villa went round the world. So did the story of *The Playboy Prince Who Gave Up His Title For Love*.

And so, too, did the next set of photos that Jean-Paul came to take.

The ones of Signor and Signora Enrico Ceraldi, with Master Benedetto Ceraldi, posing in the gardens of their two favourite residences—the newly christened Villa Elisabetta on the exclusive Capo d'Angeli estate in Italy, and the newly restored slate-roofed Cornish cottage, against whose porch leant two surfboards. One fast and mean for Signor Ceraldi, and a junior-sized one for Master Benedetto. Signora Ceraldi's surfboard was in storage, awaiting such time as Master Benedetto's new brother or sister made his expected appearance—which, as could clearly be seen from the especially voluptuous figure of Signora Ceraldi, around which Signor Ceraldi was curving a lovingly protective hand, would not be long.

As for Master Benedetto, he was sitting cross-legged on the grass and attacking a heavily defended cardboard fort with an army of brightly coloured knights in armour. His smile was almost bigger than his face.

The smile of a happy child with a happy family.

The greatest gift of all.

MILLS & BOON®

Live the emotion

JANUARY 2007 HARDBACK TITLES

ROMANCE™

Royally Bedded, Regally Wedded *Julia James*	0 263 19556 2
The Sheikh's English Bride *Sharon Kendrick*	0 263 19557 0
Sicilian Husband, Blackmailed Bride *Kate Walker*	0 263 19558 9
At the Greek Boss's Bidding *Jane Porter*	0 263 19559 7
The Spaniard's Marriage Demand *Maggie Cox*	0 263 19560 0
The Prince's Convenient Bride *Robyn Donald*	0 263 19561 9
One-Night Baby *Susan Stephens*	0 263 19562 7
The Rich Man's Reluctant Mistress *Margaret Mayo*	
	0 263 19563 5
Cattle Rancher, Convenient Wife *Margaret Way*	0 263 19564 3
Barefoot Bride *Jessica Hart*	0 263 19565 1
Their Very Special Gift *Jackie Braun*	0 263 19566 X
Her Parenthood Assignment *Fiona Harper*	0 263 19567 8
The Maid and the Millionaire *Myrna Mackenzie*	0 263 19568 6
The Prince and the Nanny *Cara Colter*	0 263 19569 4
A Doctor Worth Waiting For *Margaret McDonagh*	0 263 19570 8
Her L.A. Knight *Lynne Marshall*	0 263 19571 6

HISTORICAL ROMANCE™

Innocence and Impropriety *Diane Gaston*	0 263 19748 4
Rogue's Widow, Gentleman's Wife *Helen Dickson*	0 263 19749 2
High Seas to High Society *Sophia James*	0 263 19750 6

MEDICAL ROMANCE™

A Father Beyond Compare *Alison Roberts*	0 263 19784 0
An Unexpected Proposal *Amy Andrews*	0 263 19785 9
Sheikh Surgeon, Surprise Bride *Josie Metcalfe*	0 263 19786 7
The Surgeon's Chosen Wife *Fiona Lowe*	0 263 19787 5

MILLS & BOON®

1206 Gen Std LP

Live the emotion

JANUARY 2007 LARGE PRINT TITLES

ROMANCE™

Mistress Bought and Paid For *Lynne Graham*	0 263 19415 9
The Scorsolini Marriage Bargain *Lucy Monroe*	0 263 19416 7
Stay Through the Night *Anne Mather*	0 263 19417 5
Bride of Desire *Sara Craven*	0 263 19418 3
Married Under the Italian Sun *Lucy Gordon*	0 263 19419 1
The Rebel Prince *Raye Morgan*	0 263 19420 5
Accepting the Boss's Proposal *Natasha Oakley*	0 263 19421 3
The Sheikh's Guarded Heart *Liz Fielding*	0 263 19422 1

HISTORICAL ROMANCE™

The Bride's Seduction *Louise Allen*	0 263 19379 9
A Scandalous Situation *Patricia Frances Rowell*	0 263 19380 2
The Warlord's Mistress *Juliet Landon*	0 263 19381 0

MEDICAL ROMANCE™

The Midwife's Special Delivery *Carol Marinelli*	0 263 19331 4
A Baby of His Own *Jennifer Taylor*	0 263 19332 2
A Nurse Worth Waiting For *Gill Sanderson*	0 263 19333 0
The London Doctor *Joanna Neil*	0 263 19334 9
Emergency in Alaska *Dianne Drake*	0 263 19531 7
Pregnant on Arrival *Fiona Lowe*	0 263 19532 5

0107 Gen Std HB

MILLS & BOON®

Live the emotion

FEBRUARY 2007 HARDBACK TITLES

ROMANCE™

The Marriage Possession *Helen Bianchin*   978 0 263 19572 9
The Sheikh's Unwilling Wife *Sharon Kendrick*   978 0 263 19573 6
The Italian's Inexperienced Mistress *Lynne Graham*
   978 0 263 19574 3
The Sicilian's Virgin Bride *Sarah Morgan*   978 0 263 19575 0
The Rich Man's Bride *Catherine George*   978 0 263 19576 7
Wife by Contract, Mistress by Demand *Carole Mortimer*
   978 0 263 19577 4
Wife by Approval *Lee Wilkinson*   978 0 263 19578 1
The Sheikh's Ransomed Bride *Annie West*   978 0 263 19579 8
Raising the Rancher's Family *Patricia Thayer*   978 0 263 19580 4
Matrimony with His Majesty *Rebecca Winters*   978 0 263 19581 1
In the Heart of the Outback... *Barbara Hannay*   978 0 263 19582 8
Rescued: Mother-To-Be *Trish Wylie*   978 0 263 19583 5
The Sheikh's Reluctant Bride *Teresa Southwick*
   978 0 263 19584 2
Marriage for Baby *Melissa McClone*   978 0 263 19585 9
City Doctor, Country Bride *Abigail Gordon*   978 0 263 19586 6
The Emergency Doctor's Daughter *Lucy Clark* 978 0 263 19587 3

HISTORICAL ROMANCE™

A Most Unconventional Courtship *Louise Allen* 978 0 263 19751 8
A Worthy Gentleman *Anne Herries*   978 0 263 19752 5
Sold and Seduced *Michelle Styles*   978 0 263 19753 2

MEDICAL ROMANCE™

His Very Own Wife and Child *Caroline Anderson*
   978 0 263 19788 4
The Consultant's New-Found Family *Kate Hardy*
   978 0 263 19789 1
A Child to Care For *Dianne Drake*   978 0 263 19790 7
His Pregnant Nurse *Laura Iding*   978 0 263 19791 4

MILLS & BOON®

0107 Gen Std LP

Live the emotion

FEBRUARY 2007 LARGE PRINT TITLES

ROMANCE™

Purchased by the Billionaire *Helen Bianchin*	978 0 263 19423 4
Master of Pleasure *Penny Jordan*	978 0 263 19424 1
The Sultan's Virgin Bride *Sarah Morgan*	978 0 263 19425 8
Wanted: Mistress and Mother *Carol Marinelli*	978 0 263 19426 5
Promise of a Family *Jessica Steele*	978 0 263 19427 2
Wanted: Outback Wife *Ally Blake*	978 0 263 19428 9
Business Arrangement Bride *Jessica Hart*	978 0 263 19429 6
Long-Lost Father *Melissa James*	978 0 263 19430 2

HISTORICAL ROMANCE™

Mistaken Mistress *Margaret McPhee*	978 0 263 19382 4
The Inconvenient Duchess *Christine Merrill*	978 0 263 19383 1
Falcon's Desire *Denise Lynn*	978 0 263 19384 8

MEDICAL ROMANCE™

The Sicilian Doctor's Proposal *Sarah Morgan*	978 0 263 19335 0
The Firefighter's Fiancé *Kate Hardy*	978 0 263 19336 7
Emergency Baby *Alison Roberts*	978 0 263 19337 4
In His Special Care *Lucy Clark*	978 0 263 19338 1
Bride at Bay Hospital *Meredith Webber*	978 0 263 19533 0
The Flight Doctor's Engagement *Laura Iding*	978 0 263 19534 7